PUFFIN BOOKS

The Druid's Tune

O. R. Melling is a young Canadian
writer presently living in Ireland and
working on a second novel. Brought
up in Regent Park and then the
Beaches of Toronto, Melling is a
graduate of Trinity College (University
of Toronto).

Journey of the

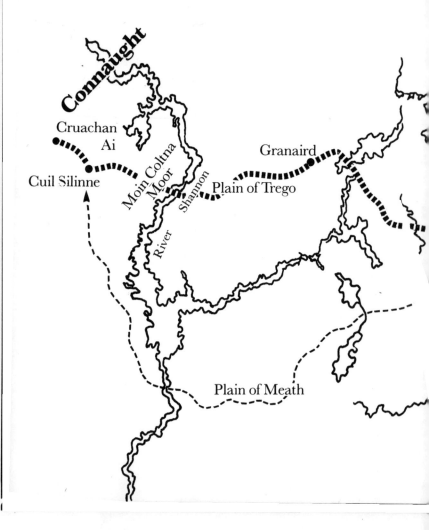

■■■■■■■ Route of Maeve's Armies

- - - - - Return Home

Connaught

Cruachan
Ai

Cuil Silinne

Moin Coltna
Moor

River Shannon

Granaird

Plain of Trego

Plain of Meath

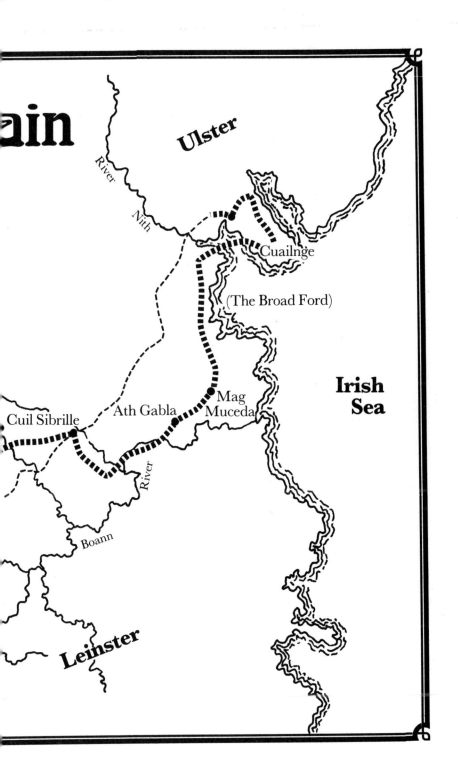

ain

Ulster

River

Nith

Cuailnge

(The Broad Ford)

**Irish
Sea**

Mag
Muceda

Cuil Sibrille   Ath Gabla

River

Boann

Leinster

The Druid's Tune
O. R. Melling

"ah, faeries dancing under the moon,
a Druid land, a Druid tune!"
W.B. Yeats

PUFFIN BOOKS

PUFFIN BOOKS

Penguin Books Ltd., Harmondsworth, Middlesex, England
Penguin Books, 40 West 23rd Street, New York, New York 10010,
U.S.A.
Penguin Books Australia Ltd., Ringwood, Victoria, Australia
Penguin Books Canada Ltd., 2801 John Street, Markham, Ontario,
Canada L3R 1B4
Penguin Books (N.Z.) Ltd., 182-190 Wairau Road, Auckland 10,
New Zealand

Published in Puffin Books, 1983

Designed by Siobhan McCooey
Manufactured in Canada by D. W. Friesen Printers

Canadian Cataloguing in Publication Data

Melling, O. R.
    The Druid's Tune

ISBN 0-14-031664-7

I. Title.

PS8576.E44D78   jC813'.54   C83-098490-9
PZ7.M44Dr

Dedication

To Peter, who was my inspiration, and to Beryl George who worked so hard for this book. My deepest thanks. And to my friends who carried me through the worst so I could be here for the best. My deepest love.

Acknowledgements

I would like to acknowledge the support and excellence of my agent, John Duff, and my editor, Cynthia Good, both of whom far extended the bounds of their professional duties for me. I am also grateful for the beautiful and conscientious work of the artist and designer, Siobhan McCooey.

Chapter One

he man chose a dark corner in the pub and pushed his knapsack under the table. He sat down quickly and hunched over his drink as if to ward off the curious stares of the townsmen. Strangers were seldom seen in Ballinamore but this man drew even more attention than most. Judging by the dusty state of his clothes and the small instrument cradled under his arm, he was a travelling musician; but though he was shabby and unkempt, his face shone pale and intelligent beneath the black frame of his hair and beard. His eyes were a startling grey colour, flickering over the room like a candle, one moment cloudy and withdrawn, the next luminous, almost white, with a strange intensity.

The townsmen disliked him instantly, though they weren't sure why, and without so much as the customary nod and "good-day", they turned their backs on him and resumed their conversations. Standing at the bar, Patsy shook his head a little sadly. He liked the looks of the man and hoped there might be a song or story to hear. Patsy's farm was more than a mile from the town but he would walk the distance after a day's work to have a quiet drink and collect the news. If he were lucky, something interesting might happen, something to think about when he was working in the fields all day. He nodded to the barman for two pints of beer and carried them over to the stranger. The man glared up at him, but Patsy placed the drinks on the table and sat down.

"Ye needn't talk to me if ye don't want," he said easily. "I'm on my way home anyways and won't be botherin' ye long."

The stranger looked him over carefully, then relaxed, and Patsy knew he was accepted as company.

"Ye've been travelling, I'd say."

"I have. For many years now," the man said.

Patsy hardly had time to note the pleasant lilt of his voice, when the man suddenly stiffened and glared at the men at the bar.

"Fools!" he hissed. "What do they think they are talking about?"

His face was contorted with fury and the harsh change in his manner gave Patsy a start. The farmer leaned forward to listen to John-Joe McGovern arguing with a friend.

"Go'way now, Ben, ye're coddin' yerself. The bull was brown like the old book says," John-Joe repeated with his usual air of absolute knowledge.

"And I say it was red. Red as blood," his friend contended.

"Oh do ye now?" John-Joe said with a look of mischief. "And would ye say the Great Queen had a red bull to match the colour of her *hair*? Is that what ye're sayin'?"

The other men burst out laughing even as Patsy did. He knew they were arguing about an old legend of the area, and that this particular subject was a favourite of John-Joe's and Ben's, a regular contest of wits that amused them and anyone else who listened.

Patsy turned back to the stranger in surprise.

"Sure it's only talk. A bit of crack."

"Talk? They can make a joke of things they know nothing about? They laugh in their own ignorance, these little men of the house and pavement..." He would have continued but for the slow hardening of Patsy's eyes.

"Ye're speakin' badly of people who have done ye no harm," the farmer said quietly.

The stranger turned away and drank his beer moodily. He began to mutter under his breath. Patsy sat back feeling slightly annoyed with him, but after awhile his annoyance switched to John-Joe and Ben. They *were* talking a lot of rubbish, he thought to himself, and the more it went on the more it bothered him. He began to feel restless, and he looked out the window at the darkening streets and decided to head home.

"Would ye's ever give over," the barman suddenly said in a loud voice. "Talk about the weather, for godsakes, and be done with it."

A silence settled over the pub and the barman looked ashamed. He never told his customers to keep quiet and had no idea why he did it now. He was about to stammer apologies when John-Joe recovered enough to comment on the long hours of the publican and how they affected a man's good nature. Everyone chuckled and John-Joe received a drink on the house, but when the talk began again it was about the town festival and their hopes for sunshine that week.

Patsy finished his drink and stood up to leave, when the stranger held his arm.

"I'm sorry for my rudeness. I am too quick in my judgements of people."

"Perhaps ye shouldn't be judgin' people at'all," Patsy said, but he was surprised by the man's sudden change of heart. A thought flashed through his mind, a quick suspicion. It was too ridiculous, and he dismissed it, but his curiosity was overwhelming him and he felt himself drawing closer to the man till he was sitting down once more.

"I'm looking for work here," the stranger said, staring hard at the farmer's face. "I want to stay here."

Patsy's eyes widened. He began to feel uneasy.

"Here? Ye must be daft! This is a poor town in the poorest county of Ireland. There's little enough work for the men here let alone a newcomer. What would a young man...?"

Patsy stopped. Was he a young man? At first he had struck him as a lad of about twenty, but now Patsy realized he couldn't begin to guess at an age. Just like his eyes, the stranger's face seemed to shift and change. Youth and something indefinably old moved together in the shadow of his features. Patsy's uneasiness grew. There was something here that he didn't know or understand. It was like the queer feeling he got sometimes when he stayed out in the fields or by Lake Drumoor too long.

"I don't want to live in the town," the man said abruptly.

Patsy saw what was coming and spoke hurriedly.

"I'm a small farmer, thirty acres of land and most of that

wild, for the cattle. I've no children, but my relations are comin' from America for the holidays. That'll be two more mouths to be feedin' and four hands to put to work. I've little money to be hirin' a man."

The stranger seemed to struggle with himself and it was some time before he could speak again.

"No, farmer, not you," he said wearily. "I'll not force you. I can only try to make you understand. I want no wages, only food and lodging. I will leave you alone and keep to myself. You won't know I'm there, but for the work done. I *need* this. I need to be near the hills."

Patsy began to feel sorry for the man and to think seriously of hiring him. He could do with the extra hand, especially if he didn't have to pay him... but why? There were too many questions to ask and he wasn't a man who liked to pry.

"I'll give ye a chance," he decided suddenly. "God knows if it's hills ye want, there's plenty on my land. They'll break your back while ye work them. And if times allow, we'll find ye a wage somewheres. I don't like to be takin' a man's labour without payin' him for it."

Patsy was embarrassed by the look on the man's face. ("Ye'd think I'd saved him from death," he said to his wife later.) He wondered again what this strange man could want with him and his farm, but the decision had been made and he put out his hand.

"My name's Patrick Donovan, 'Patsy' they call me."

"I am Peter Murphy," was all the stranger said.

The runway lights blurred into a long, shining snake as the

plane lifted from the ground and climbed into the sky. Rosemary pressed her face to the small, cool window and looked down on the city beneath her.

"We're off. No turning back now," she said lightly, but her brother heard the catch in her voice.

"It's only for a month or two," Jimmy said soothingly. "Wait and see. You'll like it once we get there."

She was hardly comforted. "How could Dad be so mean?" she wailed. "Summertime. Sending us away in the summertime!"

It was all quickly fading behind her now. Summer in Toronto with her friends—the beach, bonfires in the sand, Robert in his faded jeans playing the guitar while the water lapped against their feet.

"Bob," she said sadly.

"Oh come off it," Jimmy said. "You've only been going out with him for a month. Anyway, if it wasn't for lover-boy we wouldn't be in this mess right now."

"Shut up," his sister said. She didn't like to be reminded of that fact.

Their father had never approved of their new friends and when a few of them, including Bob, appeared in court before him one day, the matter was clinched. Jimmy was content to stay away from them, but Rosemary refused to stop seeing her boyfriend, and scene followed scene in the Redding household till their father made a final and drastic decision.

"I'm sending you to your Uncle Patsy in Ireland. Clean air, hard work, and a good, simple way of life should keep you out of mischief for a while. I have arranged everything. Your brother will go with you. I don't like to take such a hard stand, but I've seen the consequences of letting young people go their own way with bad friends. Maybe you'll come back a little wiser."

"Wiser," Rosemary thought in disgust. "How could anyone get wiser on a pokey little farm in the middle of nowhere?"

Her brother smiled as he watched the stewardess hurry gracefully down the aisle.

"You never can tell, Ro, what treasures the country might have to offer. Take haystacks, for instance. I've heard it's great in haystacks."

"Is that all you ever think about? For a fifteen-year-old you sure have a one-track mind."

"And for a seventeen-year-old you're more like an old lady," he answered with a grin. "Anyway," he said, as he leaned back and closed his eyes, "I'm going to enjoy this holiday if it kills me."

Chapter Two

 osemary woke slowly and stared around the strange room. It was bright with sunlight and the yellow walls glowed warm and golden. A high wooden wardrobe leaned against the wall and a wash-stand with jug and basin stood near her bed. The roof sloped down towards a single window, and she could see out the fluttering lace curtains to green fields and a blue sky beyond.

"Oh yes," she smiled, now fully awake. She was in her uncle's house. They had arrived in the early evening, exhausted from all their travel; the long wait at the airport, the train-ride into the heart of the countryside, and finally, a farmhouse kitchen with tea and hot scones, and their aunt and uncle laughing and talking. Ella and Patsy were quite young, she remembered, and they spoke in a funny way that somehow made them more friendly and likeable. Perhaps the holiday would not be so bad after all. She jumped out of bed and dressed quickly, heading downstairs and into the kitchen just as Jimmy walked in the door.

"How did you like sleeping in the barn?" she asked him.

"Great," he said, picking at the bits of hay in his hair. "But wait till you hear this…"

He stopped talking as their aunt Ella came in, her arms piled high with clothes.

"Here ye's are now," she said. "I'll have breakfast ready in no time. Rashers and eggs and a big pot of tea. Put the kettle on, Rose, that's a good girl. Did ye's sleep well?"

"Like a log," Rosemary answered. She looked at the table set for two. "Are we eating alone?"

Ella laughed. "Sure we've been up for hours. Patsy's at the work and I'm near finished my washin'."

They sat down feeling rather guilty as Ella cooked their meal.

"No mind," she said kindly. "Patsy says ye can have a holiday today. You'll be gettin' used to the early hours soon enough," and she left them alone.

"Getting up early on our summer holidays," Jimmy groaned.

He helped himself to more bread.

"That's the worst of it," Rosemary agreed. "But all in all it's not too bad here. Ella and Patsy aren't what I expected."

Jimmy looked around to make sure no one could hear.

"The aunt and uncle are okay," he said in a low voice, "but the hired hand is something else."

"Who?"

"This other guy who's sleeping in the barn. I guess he works here. What a weirdo! When I climbed up beside him last night and introduced myself, he gave me a look that could kill and moved his sleeping bag down to the bottom."

Rosemary shrugged. "Maybe he doesn't like 'Americans' as they call us here."

"That's what I thought...till I woke up in the middle of the night." He was whispering now. "Strange sounds woke me up."

"Don't be so silly. It was probably mice or chickens or something."

"Some farm-girl you'll make. They lock the chickens up at night. Anyway, these weren't animal noises. *He* was making them. Muttering and singing. I saw him too. Turned round in my blankets and got a sneak peek over the edge of the loft. He was playing some kind of instrument, one of those little things, not a banjo..."

"Mandolin?"

"I think so. Anyway, he was crooning to himself and rocking back and forth, crying and moaning. Really weird. Then he picked up his knapsack and left the barn. I climbed down to see where he was going—up the big hill in the back of the house. I stayed awake for at least an hour but no sign of him."

Rosemary thought it over, then started to laugh.

"Okay, I fell for it. Ver-y funny."

"I'm not kidding, honest!"

She kept laughing and shaking her head, till he left the table in disgust.

"What's wrong with him?" she thought. "He's not usually so touchy. Must be jet-lag," she decided, and she cleaned away the dishes and went outside to find her aunt.

They had seen little when they arrived in the dark of night and now Rosemary looked about her curiously.

The old farmhouse was bright and cheerful with its fresh coat of whitewash. Geraniums blossomed in the window-boxes and wisps of smoke trailed from the stone chimney.

Chickens chased each other noisily across the yard. An aging sheep-dog dozed in the shade of the rust-coloured barn. All around were the hills of Leitrim, falling gently past the pillar-posts at the end of the driveway, and rising up again behind the house and barn. She was in the heart of the hills, she realized, and she took a deep breath of the cool, refreshing air.

"I'll help," said Rosemary, running over to where her aunt stood on tiptoes at the washing-line.

"Don't you mind me," Ella said, as the white bedsheets billowed around her. "This is your day for a rest. Go on down to Lake Drumoor. It's over the hill there and through the fields. Patsy's got some fishin' rods in the press in the kitchen. Take your brother. Go on now and enjoy yourselves."

Jimmy was nowhere to be found and Rosemary decided she would do some painting instead. She unpacked her paintbox and a jar of brushes, and set out over the hill at the back of the house. As she trudged up the hill, it occurred to her that this was the way the hired hand had gone according to Jimmy. She shook her head. It would be impossible at night. The ground was wet and boggy, and potted with holes. Once up the hill, she had to climb through the briars that blocked each field like a fence. She managed the first with only a few scratches. The meadow sloped with the hill and the grass was so long her jeans were soaked to the knees.

"This lake had better be worth it," she thought, scrambling through another hedge.

"Oh no!"

Rosemary looked in dismay at the spinney of small tangled trees that crawled across the meadow and down to the lake. She could barely see the thin glimmer of the water that lay below her on the other side.

"I've come this far, might as well finish," she decided, and she plunged into the thicket with a loud crackling of dried twigs and broken branches.

Once inside, the spinney seemed larger, like a miniature forest. Tricklets of water running down from the meadow had left a pleasant carpet of soft moss. It was a lovely place filled with a green stillness and the hushed rippling of the water streams. She took her time wandering through it, and when she broke from the trees the lake spread out before her in sudden grandeur.

Lake Drumoor lay in a comfortable hollow of green hills and fields, and yet it was neither comfortable nor placid itself. The water tossed restlessly against the wild reeds and rushes, and a grey mist shimmered over the surface like a cloak. Old broken trees cowered at the edges and a damp chill smothered the sunlight. Rosemary shivered, listening nervously to the whispers of the water and the reeds.

"A wild and secret place," she thought.

She hurried over to the wooden dock and began her work. She was lost in the pale colours of the scene, and she splashed her paints in moody excitement. Time passed and the stillness welled around her like a slow ancient air.

A heavy crackling noise pulled her out of her reverie.

"Oh!" she cried, looking up.

A tall black-haired man stood over her.

"I'm not trespassing," she hurried to explain, then she realized that he must be the man who upset her brother.

He stared down at her painting and for a moment she thought he was going to say something, but with a sudden snort he left her and walked off in long strides towards the spinney. She watched him till he disappeared into the trees.

"On second thought, Jim," she said under her breath, "I don't think you were making it up after all."

She tore a page from her pad and hurriedly sketched him. When she was finished, she looked at the picture perplexed. She almost had him... but there was something missing. She dabbed some colour onto it.

"That's it!" she cried, tapping at the face she had drawn. "White highlights on grey! But how can you have eyes that colour?"

And the look in those eyes. Frightening. It was stamped all over his face. What did it mean?

"Here you are!"

She let out a yelp as Jimmy came up behind her.

"Bad nerves, eh?" he laughed.

"Actually I just met your friend," she said drily.

"Who? Oh, the mystery man in the barn?"

He plopped down beside her on the dock and arranged the fishing gear he had brought from the house.

"I bet that was fun. Did he say anything?"

"No. Just growled and stormed off."

She showed him the picture.

"That's him all right. He looks even worse at night."

Jimmy cast his line over the lake and began reeling it in. Rosemary went back to her original sketch, but couldn't keep her mind on it. She chewed on the end of her paintbrush thoughtfully.

"Jim?"

"Hmm?"

"Sorry for laughing at you. I really thought you were

pulling my leg. What do you think's the matter with him?"

"Forget about it, Ro. For now anyway."

She looked out at the lake and back behind her to the spinney and the meadows that led to the farmhouse.

"He must have come down here," she said softly. "Down to the lake."

"We'll see," was all her brother said.

That night at supper, Jimmy asked their uncle about the hired hand. Patsy stopped eating and gave him a hard look.

"Is he botherin' ye's?"

"No," Jimmy hesitated, "I was just curious about him."

Patsy sighed, "Peter Murphy's his name, and to tell ye the truth, lad, that's all I know about him. I don't go about lookin' into other people's business," he added.

"But he couldn't have appeared from nowhere?" Jimmy persisted.

Ella leaned over to pour the tea.

"Sure and he did," she said with a laugh. "Patsy's no worse at findin' lost souls than he is at pickin' up stray animals. The poor man needed work and a place to live. He's not one for mixin', but he's a good lad, quiet and polite, and no bother at'all."

"Aye, and he works hard," Patsy said. "He's a queer one all right. Won't eat with us, barely a word out of him, but ye can't hold it against a man if he wants to keep his own company."

Rosemary was following the conversation with growing interest.

"Have you ever heard him play? Jimmy says he has a mandolin."

Ella's face changed and she seemed shy to answer.

"I did," she said softly. "One day when he was in the barn and thought no one was about. At first," and she smiled a little, "I was thinkin' it was the fairies. It was so sweet and so sad. He wouldn't play for ye, mind. I never asked him, but I'm sure of it."

Later, when their aunt and uncle had gone to bed, Rosemary and Jimmy sat in front of the fire with cups of cocoa.

"There's something about that man," Jimmy said. "I don't know how or why, but he's getting to me. I'd like to find out what he's up to."

"You sound like one of the Hardy boys," Rosemary said. "You're being ridiculous." But she didn't sound too sure.

Jimmy stared into the fire with a determined look.

"There's one way to find out. We can follow him."

"Oh no you don't," his sister began. "I'm not sneaking out of the house in the middle of the night. Besides, I wouldn't *want* to run into him in the dark."

"For the first point I could put the barn ladder up to your window. You're nowhere near Ella and Patsy's room. And for the second," he gave her a sly look, "I've never known you to be afraid of anything or anyone."

"You're playing dirty," she said, but she didn't want to look like a coward. "Okay. If he makes a move, come and get me. But you'd better not make any noise, because if you get caught I know nothing."

"That a girl, sis. I'm sure this Peter Murphy won't disappoint us. See you later."

He went out to the barn whistling happily. Rosemary turned out the lights and went thoughtfully up to her room.

As she undressed, she left her jeans and boots where she

could reach them easily, and as an afterthought, she opened her window halfway.

"I must be crazy," she thought, climbing into bed.

But she couldn't help feeling excited and she fell asleep hoping something would happen. When the tapping on her window began, she was up in an instant.

Chapter Three

he tapping sounds were followed by loud whispers as Jimmy poked his head into her room. Rosemary motioned to him to keep quiet and he disappeared again. She dressed stealthily and tiptoed to the window. The night was crisp and still. Without clouds to hide them, the stars and the moon shone white and clear. The yard was flooded with light and the barn loomed over it huge and dark. Jimmy stood at the bottom waving her on, and she climbed out the window and hurried down the ladder.

"We've got to get moving," Jimmy urged. "He's already up the hill and out of sight."

"We can't leave the ladder against the house," she whispered, looking around nervously.

When they finally set out, Jimmy cursed himself for not thinking of a flashlight. Despite the moon it was rough-going uphill and they kept slipping on the damp grass and stumbling into holes. Every now and then a cow in a neighbouring field would let out a low, mournful cry and the two would jump in fear. Both had the same thought in their

minds. If he came back now, they had nowhere to hide.
They thought they would never reach the shelter of the
hedges.

"What's that noise?"

Jimmy clutched his sister's arm. Panic rose to choke her.

"Can you hear it? It's going 'boom-boom, boom-boom'."

Rosemary gave him a push.

"That's your heart thumping, you dummy."

With much relief they reached the hedgerow of the first
meadow and crouched under the bushes, thankful for cover.
They scanned the dim field. Trees creaked in the night wind
and shadows dappled the grass, but they could see no one.

"I think we should make a run for it," Jimmy said,
though he didn't like the idea. He looked across the length
of the field. The hedge on the other side seemed miles away.
By the moonlight, they would easily be seen in the open.

But his sister agreed. "If we stick to the bushes we'll never
catch up with him."

They dashed out into the meadow, not daring to stop or
look around. At last they were scrambling beneath the
hawthorn once again. Bits of branches and twigs tickled
their faces and Jimmy suddenly sneezed. The fright he gave
both of them sent him into a fit of giggles and he clapped his
hand over his mouth.

"Knock it off," Rosemary hissed. "He could be nearby."

"I can't help it," he whispered back, muffling a fresh set
of laughs.

"If he catches us, I'll kill you."

Rosemary pushed aside the tangle of branches to survey
the second meadow. She caught her breath. There was a
tall shape standing darkly against the moonlit spinney.

"He's wearing a cloak!" she told Jimmy. "What on earth is he up to?"

"Curiouser and curiouser," Jimmy said, leaning over her to see. "There, he's gone, into the trees!"

For one long moment they froze in doubt. Did they really want to follow him? Did they really want to know what he was doing?

Jimmy decided first.

"Don't chicken out now," he whispered, and he pinched her before starting off.

They hunched down in the high grass, half-crawling, half-running, hoping desperately that eyes were not watching from the thicket. The ground was wet and mucky with the water running downhill to the lake. The soft sucking noises of their feet in the mud unnerved them. They crept quickly into the trees, barely breathing as they held onto the withered trunks for support. Deep inside the spinney, they stopped to listen.

"I don't hear him," Rosemary said, putting her lips to Jimmy's ear.

"He's too quiet. We've got to look for him," Jimmy answered the same way.

They were on their hands and knees, oblivious to the cold, drenched earth. Their eyes slowly grew accustomed to the dimness and they moved cautiously, peering through the branches and around the twisted tree trunks. Eyes and ears were strained to catch a glimpse or the slightest sound.

Rosemary gasped as a cold finger prodded her arm.

"Just ahead," Jimmy hissed.

There amidst the trees was a shape too dark to be the night air. A rustling noise, and it was gone. The chase had begun. It soon struck them as they ran that the spinney had suddenly grown immense, but they didn't stop to wonder. They were bent on one object, to keep the man in sight. They clambered over rocks and patches of briar and gorse, slid down banks and splashed through streams. Their faces and hands were scratched, their breathing quick and painful, but still they followed him. He moved like a creature of the night, swift and silent. They never caught more than the dark flash of his cloak or a sudden silhouette in a moment of light. At times they wondered if the darkness was playing tricks on them. What had they seen against the tree that time? A white claw? And when the moonlight shone through a gap in the bushes hadn't they seen something far bigger than Peter, just for a second? Their fear was growing steadily, but they had no thoughts of giving up or going back. It was as if they were driven in their pursuit of him.

"Be...careful," Jimmy gasped, as they stopped to catch their breath. They pressed their faces to a cool, damp tree. "I see light ahead...could be the field or the lake...he might...see us."

They crept carefully toward the light and came out of the trees. Lake Drumoor lay before them, smooth and icy, like a sheet of stained glass. The grey water had taken on a silver tinge and it glistened eerily in the pallid moonlight.

Rosemary put her hand to her mouth to stop the scream.

By the shore of the cold lake, his cloak flowing from him like black water, lay the man Peter. The wind tossed back the hair from his forehead and they could see his eyes, fixed and staring at the sky. Eyes as white and dead as the moon that stared back.

"He must be insane," Rosemary whispered, her voice shaking.

She felt ashamed as well as frightened. Somehow it wasn't right. They shouldn't be there to witness his madness.

"Come on. Let's go," Jimmy said, taking her hand.

But even as they turned to leave, they froze in new terror. Screams rose behind them, shattering the silence of the night. Wild, inhuman screams. Rosemary fell to her knees in a near faint. She could sense Jimmy beside her but she wasn't able to move or speak. She closed her eyes, begging that it would stop. When the cries ended, they lay on the grass shaking with relief, but the silence was short, and the man began to call out in a voice that was hoarse with pain and breath—

"I see it!
Sacred tree of the fire.
Blood pours from the knotted
trunk of the tree!
I see it!

I see it!
Ravens sitting on the branch,
A plain red-blooded beneath the sun,
Black furies swirling,
The red-mouth screeching.
I see it!"

The shouts turned into a mumbling and tumbling of strange words that droned into the night. Rosemary felt her fear subsiding as exhaustion washed over her. She dragged herself from the ground and reached out for Jimmy. His body lay motionless beside her, but she was too dizzy to move him. She fell back unconscious.

Fast asleep, the two couldn't see the change that took place. Nor did they see Peter stand up and raise his arms to the sky in silent gratitude. He was about to leave when he noticed them curled up together and sleeping peacefully. He stood over them, shocked and furious. Then he sighed.

"Of course. Three of us. Why didn't I think of that before?"

He looked down at them and shock his head. Who would ever have thought? Two foreigners. Ignorant children. Still, he had felt that this place was right. He stooped to pick up his knapsack, and hoisting it on his shoulders, he left them.

Chapter Four

hen Jimmy woke, he found himself blinking from the hard glare of the sun. He was up in an instant, and by the time his vision cleared the shock had settled into reality. The lake and the field were gone. Around him spread a level plain. Mountains gleamed in the distance.

"I must be dreaming," he said out loud.

Rosemary groaned beside him and stood up shakily.

"I see you're in my dream too," he said in a funny voice.

"What do you mean *your* dream?" she demanded in bewilderment.

An argument began over whose dream it was and whether or not it was a dream, and they pinched each other to see if they could wake up.

"That feels real enough to me," said Jimmy, rubbing the red mark on his arm.

They were beginning to calm down and talk sensibly when a high, piercing sound echoed over the plain.

"Over there!" Jimmy cried, pointing to a thin dark line that moved quickly towards them.

At first they could see nothing but a thick cloud of dust. Then a steady drumming noise reached their ears and the ground trembled beneath them.

"Horses," Rosemary whispered. "I hope they're not stampeding."

But as the great steeds rode into sight, they saw the riders; men tall against the horizon with hair and cloaks streaming behind them. The high winding call sounded again, and Rosemary and Jimmy knew that the riders had sighted them. With nowhere to hide, they could only stand there till they were surrounded.

"Who are you?" Rosemary said in amazement.

She had never seen men like these before. Cloaks of green and brown fell from their broad shoulders and every hand gripped a round shield and an evil-looking spear. Beneath the thick yellow hair, eyes glinted hard and wild. One of the men rode near and peered down at Rosemary. Unlike the rest, he was clean-shaven and even pleasant-looking, and she was surprised to see that he was no older than herself. Nonetheless his blond-red hair was bound with a golden circlet and he was obviously the leader. He suddenly smiled at her and his eyes were bright with humour and curiosity.

"It is hardly your place to question *us*, girl."

He reached out to touch her hair.

"Hair like the night... and such strange clothing. But you are fair-faced. Whose slave might you be?"

"There's no slavery in our country," Jimmy blurted out. He didn't like the way the man was looking at his sister and he was growing more nervous by the minute.

"It's no country that we know of then," one of the riders said, lifting his spear. He looked towards the leader. "Shall we kill them, Maine?"

Before Rosemary or Jimmy could move, the spear stood quivering in the ground between them. The other men raised their weapons.

"If this is a dream," Jimmy muttered, "I'd like to wake up just about now."

"No, I think not," said Maine, still smiling at Rosemary. "They do not have the look of spies. It would be unwise to shed innocent blood before the battle starts. We will take them back to the Queen."

He winked at his men as he lifted Rosemary to the saddle.

"I'll take the pretty maiden. You take the boy, Conn."

Their journey was swift and uneventful. The steady beat of the horses' hooves was the only sound to disturb the quiet of the countryside. Rosemary looked at the green hills and plains that rose and fell around her, but nothing was familiar. She leaned against her captor to keep out of the wind and felt oddly reassured by his solid warmth. When they stopped on a height overlooking a vast, rolling plain, Maine pointed below.

"Cruachan Ai," he said proudly.

Upon the great plain below them spread a black mass of tents and men, horses and chariots. Hardly a blade of grass was visible and the low roar of the huge gathering reached them even at their distance.

"But what? Who?" Rosemary stammered. "What's going on?"

Unable to see her face, Maine chuckled.

"Very wise, stranger, to pretend you know nothing of the preparations for war. But lies are unnecessary. This hosting can no longer be kept secret. Rumours and messages have been flying about the country for weeks."

"We just got here yesterday," Rosemary said in confusion.

Her words were lost in a blast of sound as the riders wound their horns. Maine gave the signal to move and they rode recklessly down the hill and onto the plain.

The camp was a tumult of noise and movement. There were warriors everywhere, on horseback and in chariot, practise-fighting with sword and spear, or leaning on their weapons in noisy groups. They exchanged shouts and insults with the red-faced camp-women who worked over boiling pots and smoky fires. Servants rushed about, their arms laden with food and wood. Children and dogs, each as grubby as the other, played in and out of the crowd, dodging slaps and curses. The air was thick with the odours of sweat and dung, smoking wood, and haunches of roast meat. Rosemary was stunned. There seemed to be thousands upon thousands of people and animals.

They rode quickly through the congested area till they reached the heart of the camp where there were fewer tents and less people. Here the soldiers appeared to be older and more restrained, and gold and silver flashed on the bodies of both men and women. They drew up to the largest tent of all, a giant oblong structure of hide and wood. Armed men stood guard outside and they raised their weapons in salute as Maine jumped from his horse and swung Rosemary to the ground. By this time Rosemary knew Maine was someone important and she was glad to have a protector in this war-like place. She smiled sweetly up at him.

"Thanks for saving my brother and me."

"Your skin isn't safe yet," he replied seriously, "but if you must be killed, I shall do it myself. Cleanly and swiftly."

"Thanks a lot."

He laughed at her dry tone and gave her nose a tweak.

"I would rather kiss you than kill you, though."

"Of all the nerve," she thought, following him into the tent, but the idea appealed to her all the same.

Jimmy was pushed in behind her looking none too pleased. They found themselves in a wide room crowded with tall, grey-haired men who had the look and bearing of leaders. But it wasn't at the men that Rosemary and Jimmy stared in awe. Before them stood a huge woman, tall and broad, with a face as cold and imperious as the heavy jewels that adorned her. She was dressed in wild and vivid colours, and against the bright cloth of her mantle her hair gleamed a dark, metallic red. She towered over everyone and everything in the room.

"I have two curiosities for you, mother," Maine said.

The Queen's eyes darkened with anger and impatience as she looked down at the ruffled intruders.

"What clothing is this?" she demanded, striding over to Rosemary and pulling roughly at her jeans. "Leggings on a girl?"

Rosemary didn't look happy but she kept her mouth shut.

"Not of our people," the Queen said scornfully, pointing to the black hair of both sister and brother. "They could be spies from Ulster."

"We're from Canada," Jimmy said, a little too loudly, and when she glared at him he added, "Ma'am."

"Never heard of the place."

She turned to one of her attendants. "Fetch a Druid. I have enough problems with this infernal delay, I have no time for strangelings. They can be sacrificed for good luck."

"Now just a minute," Rosemary and Jimmy said.

"Silence!" roared the Queen.

They swallowed their protests and looked at each other horrified. Things were going from bad to worse and they couldn't begin to understand what was going on.

"We need advice, Druid," the Queen said over their heads as someone entered the tent.

Despite her orders and their own fear, Rosemary and Jimmy let out a cry as the man walked in front of them.

"Peter!"

Chapter Five

n their relief at seeing a familiar face, Rosemary and Jimmy could have hugged the man, but his appearance hardly allowed for that. Leaves and white berries were tangled in his mass of dark hair. Both his cloak and gown were black as the night. A band of gold coiled around his neck, casting a yellowish sheen over his long, sharp face; but the glimmer of light did not warm the wintry gaze of his grey eyes. He ignored them and turned to the Queen.

"What is it you want, Maeve?"

"These children have appeared from nowhere and claim they are not of Ulster. They seem to know you? Should they be put to death?"

"I am Peadar Murricu," he said to them, as if he didn't recognize them. "I am a priest of the Druithin. I have the *imbas forasnai*, the Light of Foresight, and the power to see truth."

They were too surprised to say anything and he spoke again to the Queen.

"They are not of you or against you. They are the sign.

The sign that the armies may cease their lingering and commence the march.''

Maeve clapped her hands in delight.

"We leave at dawn!" she cried to her chieftains, and the men rushed from the tent, shouting orders and creating an uproar outside.

The Druid slipped away as the Queen regarded Rosemary and Jimmy in a less unfriendly manner.

"You are welcome in my camp," she said, and the two breathed freely now that the talk of killing was over.

"We have been kept here a fortnight," Maeve went on. "The Druids demanded a sign before we could move. It is well that you have begun this invasion, but I have no wish for strangers in my company. You," she said to Jimmy, "find Fergus mac Roich and tell him I have sent you to join him."

Rosemary and Jimmy exchanged glances. They didn't like the idea of separating, but the Queen was waiting impatiently.

"I'll look out for you," Jimmy said hurriedly, and he left the tent.

Holding Rosemary by the arm, Maeve followed him outside. She scanned the crowd which was even livelier and noisier than before and called out to a young girl surrounded by chattering women.

"Finnabar! Take this girl and have her clothed properly. Keep her in your care till I send for her."

With that the Queen shouted for her horse, and climbing onto it with shield and spear in hand, she cried out triumphantly.

"Wives and lovers will curse my name this day, for I have gathered their men to invade Ulster!"

The way was quickly cleared as she galloped through the camp and Rosemary looked after her with mingled awe and dislike.

"Don't mind my mother," a voice said behind her. "She thrives on all this. War and slaughter and glory."

Finnabar had little resemblance to the Queen. Her face was gentle and pretty beneath the pale yellow hair and her blue eyes were warm with laughter. She moved with a languid, easy grace, linking her arm in Rosemary's as they walked.

"So what do you like?" Rosemary asked, thinking the girl a welcome change from her mother.

"Oh, cloths of rose and flowered linen and shy men," she laughed. "Mother is disgusted with me. I have no heart for killing. But what horrible things you are wearing, if you don't mind me saying so."

"I don't mind," Rosemary said. She looked with envy at the girl's soft gown and the bright stones that sparkled on her arms and throat. "Then why are you on this invasion or whatever it is, if you don't like war?"

Finnabar smiled ruefully. "It's hardly a question of choice. Mother has promised me to seven kings so they will bring their armies to join her."

Rosemary was shocked. "You didn't have any say in the matter?"

"Certainly not. She is the Queen and my mother."

"But you won't have to marry any of them?"

Finnabar was amused. "Of course I will. Whoever survives I suppose. If more than one survives, then they fight. But you *are* strange. Why should that bother you? Don't you obey your mother?"

"Not when it comes to picking boyfriends or husbands that's for sure."

The other girl shrugged. "When you come down to it, one man is the same as another."

A merry voice chimed in behind them as Maine squeezed himself between the two girls.

"What ideas are you putting in the pretty head of my captive, dear sister?"

He winked at Rosemary and she laughed and pretended to ignore him. Finnabar raised her eyebrows at the two of them.

"You shouldn't be here, brother," she said fondly. "You should be preparing your men for the march. The strangers you brought were the sign the Druids wanted. All the camp is talking about it."

"I am well aware of that, but my men have been ready this long time past."

He slipped his arm around Rosemary's waist.

"Will you put one of your nice gowns on this girl, Finn? So I can see if she is as fair as I think?"

Rosemary tried to be angry and insulted but finally gave up. He was too handsome and charming. She couldn't help liking him.

"I'll give you a kiss when I see you next," he said.

"I see *you* don't prefer the shy ones," Finnabar teased when her brother was gone. "I have seven brothers, you know, all named Maine. Sometimes I can't tell one from the other."

"I think I could tell him from the rest," Rosemary ventured.

"Well, you have chosen the sweetest. They call him Maine Milscothach, 'of the honeyed speech'. He has fair words for all, but especially the maidens."

They came up to a small tent and Finnabar led her inside.

"This is mine," she said with a little sigh. "I only wish I was showing you my room in the palace. Please pretend you don't see the mess. I am not very tidy."

The ground was covered with fresh rushes and sweet-smelling grass. Fur mats and rich cushions were scattered about, and gowns of every cloth and colour hung from the wooden beams. There were baskets and trunks stacked haphazardly against the wall, their contents of clothes and jewellery spilling onto the floor. Finnabar looked at her dresses thoughtfully.

"We shall dress you up for Maine, then, since you like him. Which one do you want?"

While Rosemary was happily stepping into Finnabar's clothes, Jimmy was wandering about in search of the company he was to join. On the far side of the plain, outside the main camp, he was surprised to find a small army settled a deliberate distance from the rest. This camp was different, more regimented and masculine. After awhile Jimmy realized there were no women, children or servants to be seen. Every soldier seemed proud and noble and almost all wore a circlet of gold around their brows. Jimmy walked up to a tall, elderly man who was instructing two warriors in a practice-fight.

"Do you know where I can find Fergus mac Roich?" Jimmy asked him.

The man's dark eyes flashed suspiciously as he looked down. His face was hard and worn, marked with the scars of battle and age. There was an air of tired majesty in the way he held his grey head, but his body was straight and powerful. Jimmy felt suddenly aware of his own youth.

"And what, stripling, do you want with Fergus mac Roich?"

Jimmy cleared his throat. He guessed he had found his man.

"Well, sir, Queen Maeve sent me to join your company."

"You do not look like a Connaughtman," Fergus said in a distinctly unfriendly tone.

"A what, sir? We, I mean my sister and I, uh, Peter brought us here...from somewhere else. I'm Canadian, but I don't suppose that means..."

Fergus took hold of Jimmy's chin and roughly pulled him forward.

"Tell me you are not a spy of Maeve," he commanded harshly.

Jimmy's eyes widened as Fergus tightened his grip, and the boy found himself being lifted from the ground to meet the soldier's angry face.

"I'm not! Believe me, I don't even know what's going on!"

Fergus suddenly let go and his face lost its stern look.

"I believe you. You are no liar. Maeve probably sent you here in case you were one of *my* spies."

"Seems like nobody trusts anyone around here," Jimmy said, rubbing his sore chin.

The old warrior laughed. "That's the times, my lad. We are all looking out for our own skins. But what will I do with you? Hmm?"

Jimmy relaxed at Fergus's friendly tone and looked at the men who were practise-fighting with spears and swords.

"I wouldn't mind trying that," he suggested.

Fergus nodded, obviously pleased with the answer.

"Very well. We will train you in arms and you can be my charioteer. We are all warriors here and have no servants to command. Will you accept that?"

"I'd be honoured, sir," said Jimmy.

Chapter Six

 t was evening before Rosemary and Jimmy could slip away to meet. At first they hardly recognized each other. Jimmy wore a short, woven tunic and leather sandals strapped up to his knees. Grandly he swept aside his broad woollen cloak to show the sword and scabbard that hung at his side. Finnabar had given Rosemary a pale, rose-coloured gown clasped with silver brooches and a dark red mantle that fell to her feet. Her long hair was pulled back with combs of white deer-horn, and Jimmy said she looked rather good.

"See what Fergus gave me," he said, unsheathing a short, blunt sword. "It's a stabbing sword. I get to try the longer ones next. I've already had a few lessons with this." He waved the weapon over his head with new-found skill. "Tomorrow I'll be driving the chariot. Fergus says I'll be his servant-in-arms since the rest of his men are full-fledged warriors."

"This is great fun, isn't it?" Rosemary said. "I'm with Finnabar, Maeve's daughter, but she's not like her mother at all. We're best friends already."

They talked and talked, interrupting each other with stories of what they had done and seen that day.

"But what we've got to figure out," Rosemary said finally, "is where we are and how we got here. Uncle Patsy and Aunt Ella must be having a fit."

Jimmy's face fell. He hadn't thought of their aunt or uncle since the adventure began.

"Well, we're in Ireland, in Connaught—everyone says so. We can't be that far away," he said hopefully.

"Don't be ridiculous. You know this isn't the Ireland we were in before. Though I'm not sure about it, I've got an idea. Finnabar told me the Druids—you know, what Peter says he is—she says they have special powers, like wizards or magicians or something. I think this is all an illusion, or maybe a dream of Peter's and somehow we managed to get mixed up in it."

"I don't think so, Ro. This all feels very real to me."

"That's part of the magic, I suppose. Why do you think everyone here speaks English?"

"*Do* they?" Jimmy insisted. "Are we speaking English right now? Don't you get the feeling sometimes that the words you're hearing and saying are *different*?"

Rosemary thought about that for awhile. She had had the queer feeling several times during the day that the conversations around her were in a strange language even though she understood everything that was being said.

"We're in another place," Jimmy concluded. "That's all. Somewhere that Peter has brought us to, probably by magic as you say. And somehow we fit into it."

"Well, no matter," she said, now thoroughly confused. "We either have to wake up, or go back to where we came from. We'll be in awful trouble if we don't."

Jimmy stared glumly at his toes and thought about his chariot lessons. Rosemary wasn't much happier. Now that she had insisted on their leaving, she remembered Finnabar and her lovely clothes, and Maine and the kiss he had promised.

"Couldn't we stay just a little longer?" Jimmy pleaded. "We could always think up something to cover ourselves when we get back."

Though she was trying hard to be practical, Rosemary gave in without an argument. She put her hand out and Jimmy put his on top of it, something they always did when they were most likely heading for trouble.

"Agreed. We'll keep on like this for a while and take the consequences together. We'll find Peter and tell him we must go back in a day or two."

Jimmy did a little jump in the air. "Now that that's settled, will you come and meet Fergus? He wants to see you."

"Great idea. Finn has to go to the Queen's tent to comb her hair and that will get me out of the way neatly."

Happy with their decision to stay, they made their way towards Fergus' camp. Rosemary lifted her long skirts as they walked over the muddy plain and Jimmy casually chopped at the odd bush or tree with his sword. No one paid any attention to them and they chatted and laughed as they strolled along. When they reached the camp, Jimmy showed his sister the tent he shared with Fergus, and the chariot he would be driving in the morning.

"It's the finest chariot in the camp. It's mostly wood, as you can see, but the wheels are bronze and so are the studs that hold the whole thing together. The yokes and poles, there, hold the harness. These are the bits, for the horses' mouths..."

Rosemary shook her head. "But you can't even drive a car!"

He shrugged sheepishly. "Fergus is going to teach me everything he knows. He told me all kinds of things today. This isn't really a war, for instance. They call it a 'Tain', a cattle-raid. They gather as many warriors together as possible, invade someone's kingdom, and rustle off their cattle."

"Sounds like the wild west," Rosemary said, laughing.

"It is in a way. Cattle is all they're really interested in. They're not out to steal land or conquer new territory. Fergus made that clear to me. Anyway, Fergus and his men are from the Kingdom of Ulster..."

"Ulster? Isn't that the place we're attacking?"

"Sure is, and this company—see how they're separated from the rest?—this company is made up of exiles from Ulster. I don't know why they're here or raiding their own country, but Fergus promised he'd tell me tonight. Come on, they'll be in the centre of the camp."

They came to a large bonfire where the Ulstermen sat drinking and singing. Jimmy led his sister over to Fergus.

"This is Rosemary, sir. She's with Finnabar in Maeve's camp."

Fergus looked at her with calm, dark eyes.

"She is no more of Connaught than you, son, but it is well that she is with Maeve. We have no women among us and her face would be a problem."

Rosemary took this as an offhand compliment and she sat down with Jimmy at the old warrior's feet.

"I have promised you the tale of the Ulster exiles, James,"

Fergus said with a sad smile. "Do you know of Conchobor, the King of Ulster? No? Then you would not know the fate of the sons of Usna. My harper will tell it."

At a signal from Fergus, an old man stepped close to the fire. He carried a golden harp under his arm and they could see by his pale eyes that he was blind. The warriors grew silent as the harper's fingers rippled over the taut strings and a sweet, distant music filled the air. In a mellow, sing-song voice, he began to chant —

> "There was once born to Ulster's land,
> A woman foretold of perilous beauty,
> Her long dim hair would darken honour,
> Her white-necked body kill a warrior,
> Her eyes of fire would burn a king,
> And so the Druids claimed her death.
>
> Conchobor stayed the girl-child's death,
> Loving all women born to his land,
> He named her Deirdre, wife of the king,
> This island-flower and gentle beauty.
> Hidden from the sight of any warrior,
> She was locked away, for Ulster's honour.
>
> But a maiden's dream is love, not honour,
> And imprisoned life is a lover's death,
> From the high walls, she spied a warrior,
> Naoise, son of Usna, hero of the land.
> Seeing his form of youth's sweet beauty,
> She spurned the grey-haired, lonely king.
>
> Naoise feared the wrath of the king,
> But Deirdre bound him by his honour,
> He and two brothers stole the beauty,

And Conchobor plotted to have their death.
They fled from Ireland, to Alba's land,
For years he wandered, the hapless warrior.

"Forgive his deeds," said Fergus the warrior,
And seemingly so, did the dark-eyed king,
He recalled the exiles to their land,
Their safety pledged by Fergus' honour.
They returned to Ulster, no fear of death,
The three sons of Usna, and Deirdre the beauty.

Weep, weep for murdered beauty!
Trickery ruined Fergus the warrior.
The sons of Usna met their death,
By favour-seekers, friends of the king.
Weep, weep for broken honour!
Their young blood blackens the land.

She died, the beauty. And Naoise, the warrior.
Shame the King! And Fergus, his honour!
Bleed the land! Redeem by death!"

As the song ended, the men around the fire sat quiet and
unmoving. Fergus spoke in a low voice that was filled with
pain.

"I was to escort Naoise and his brothers to the court of the
King as their guarantor of safety. I was tricked from meeting
them, but I sent my son in my place. He did well. The spear
that broke Naoise's back went first through my son's heart."

He stared into the flames and some of the men muttered
in sympathy. Finally he stood up and looked around at the
company.

"Gathered here by my fire are the greatest and most
noble of Ulster's fighting men. I, Fergus mac Roich. There,

Fiacha mac Fir Febe, the son of Conchobor the King. And leaning upon his shoulder, Conall Cernach, an old veteran like myself, a man of countless battles. Since the day of that treacherous murder and the shaming of my honour, we and our men have waged war upon our homeland. I, myself, have thrice burned Emain Macha, the home of the King. For years we have lived in this hole called Connaught. Not for love of Maeve or her husband Ailill do we ride on this Tain, but for revenge on Ulster."

"Your own land," murmured Rosemary. "Your own people."

Fergus clenched his fists.

"There is nothing to the warrior that comes before his honour. Not king or home or blood. My name was given in a pledge of safety to the sons of Usna. With their death, I was shamed and my name became nothing."

When Fergus left, the group around the fire talked quietly, but soon the serious mood lifted and the harper was called upon to play more cheerful tunes. The men returned to their drinking and singing, and from the looks cast in her direction Rosemary grew aware that she was the only girl in the company. Remembering Fergus's earlier words, she whispered to Jimmy that she should be getting back.

"That was some story, eh?" Jimmy said, as they walked back to Maeve's camp.

"It's awful the way these women are forced to marry people they don't love," Rosemary said. "Finnabar is in the same position, and that poor girl, Deirdre! No wonder everyone ends up fighting."

"I don't think the girl has anything to do with why Fergus and his men are fighting," Jimmy argued. "It's not even so much that Fergus's son was killed. As far as I can see, there's a big point of honour at stake. Fergus promised the girl and the three warriors a safe arrival. When the warriors were killed and she died, all the blame was put on Fergus and he lost his honour. He couldn't stay in Ulster and he keeps attacking it in revenge."

"That sounds like a long, drawn out excuse for robbing and murdering people if you ask me," Rosemary said hotly. "And worse still, his own country."

Jimmy sighed, "I know what you're saying, Ro, but Fergus and his men aren't like that. I can tell. They're honourable people, not like Maeve and the Connaught-men."

"You can't judge a people by their leaders, Jim. The Ulster king sounds just as bad as Maeve, killing people all over the place. And besides, some of the Connaughtmen are quite nice," she added, thinking of Maine.

"Maybe so," Jimmy said, "but I'm sort of an honourary Ulsterman at the moment, so I'm on their side."

Chapter Seven

arly the next morning, Rosemary and Jimmy searched through the camp for 'Peadar Murricu.'

"The Druithin seldom ride to war," a man told them when they described Peter. "They are not bound by military law."

"Do you know where we could find him?"

"The priests have secret places that no one knows of. They wander the land and come and go as they please."

"There's nothing we can do till he comes back for us," Jimmy said with a shrug. He looked pleased though he was trying not to.

"*If* he comes for us," Rosemary said with a worried frown.

"He'll have to," Jimmy said. "After all, he's responsible for us."

They looked at each other uneasily. The Druid didn't strike them as the type of person who would recognize such a responsibility.

"We'll just have to carry on till something comes up," Rosemary sighed, "but there'll be a lot of explaining to do if this goes on for too long."

"Here you are!" cried Maine.

He strode up to them in full battle-dress with his men following close behind. With a great laugh, he lifted Rosemary into the air and gave her a long, lingering kiss. Jimmy reached for his sword but stopped when he heard his sister's laughter. Maine put her back on the ground and twirled her around in admiration.

"I didn't think you really wanted to leave," Jimmy muttered, as he watched them.

It was typical of her to find someone to fall in love with, even in this place. He shook his head. If they were to stay he had a chariot to drive, and he left to find Fergus.

"I have a gift for you," Maine said to Rosemary, "so you will not think my sister the only generous one in the family."

It was a dagger hardly bigger than her hand. The pale bronze curved like a tiny sword, graceful and deadly, and the handle shone with gold and silver flecks. She held it lightly in her palm and admired its beauty.

One of the men made a noise behind them and Maine was suddenly brusque and efficient.

"Conn, have the men form up in company behind the Ulster exiles. The Queen has named Fergus leader of the march despite my protests, so I want you to keep an eye on him and report back with anything suspicious. I'll ride with this girl as far as Mag Muceda, then I'll join you. Send Ele to me with the white mare. You can ride, Rose?"

"Not very well. I only tried it once."

"How strange. But I'll ride with you for a time. Much of the way is through our own or our allies' territory, so there'll be little need for caution till we reach Ulster."

"Is it a long journey?"

"Across the breadth of Ireland," he said grandly, but when he saw her face he added hastily, "but then, the country is no great size. Here, I'll show you."

He went down on one knee to sketch in the ground. Rosemary leaned over him to watch, and as her dark hair and red mantle trailed over his arm, he looked up at her. His face was suddenly grave.

"Long black hair and rose and silver shining," he said softly. "I'll look after you."

She felt shy and couldn't meet his eyes. He smiled and began drawing a rough map in the earth.

"This is Cruachan Ai, the plain of Connaught. Our march is to the east, to Ulster, the northeastern kingdom of Ireland. We'll go slowly at first till we find the strengths and weaknesses among the armies. Hopefully we'll reach Cuil Silinne, here, by tonight, and camp down before crossing the moor of Moin Coltna. The moor is fine ground for wild deer and it would be good to cross it slowly and hunt as we go. That will take us directly to the west bank of the River Shannon."

"What a pretty name—Shannon," Rosemary said.

"It belongs to the goddess who fought against her sister for the Salmon of Knowledge."

"Really? Who won?"

"Neither. They both drowned in the rivers named after them, the Shannon and the Boann. The Salmon of Knowledge refused to be caught by a woman."

"Hmphh," said Rosemary.

"We will have to ford the Shannon, and with our numbers and supplies it will be no easy task. Do not fear, the horses can swim and I'll help you. East again, we march to Trego, the Plain of the Spears, a bleak and windy plain that stretches for miles, then through the hills of Granaird, and a straight march to Cuil Sibrille. Let me see, south, then, and east to the plain of Mag Muceda. I shall have to leave you and join my men at that point. Ulster is not far from there and I must lead in case of attack. But we'll be in sight of the sea by then, Rose, you'll like that. Ah, the sea—Mannanan's blue cloak fringed with the white of the surf."

"Mannanan?"

"He who rules birth and rebirth. The waters of the world are his mantle. But I suppose you call your gods by different names?"

"I suppose so," said Rosemary, who didn't talk about those things. "And after that?" she prompted.

"We move up the coastland to Methe Tog, and north to the River Nith which we'll cross at Ath Lethan, the Broad Ford. That again will be a difficult crossing and we'll have to wait for low tide. Once across, we have reached our destination, the peninsula of Cuailnge. Where we go after that," he shrugged, "depends on the fighting."

Rosemary pushed the last thought out of her mind. She didn't want to think about the war they were riding to. By the time they set out on the road to Ulster, she had completely dismissed it from her mind.

The morning had slowly matured from a chilly, grey new-dawn to the full and golden splendour of day. The sun lit up the green hills and hollows of Ireland, and the birds sang in the trees that dipped over the roadway. The road was a wide dirt track cleared of undergrowth and trees, and the armies filed down it like a winding, black snake. There was a holiday air about the march, with the rhythmic creaking of the chariots and the jaunty clopping of the war-horses, the chanting of the men who marched on foot, their spears held high into the sun, and the slow, easy pace of the companies that stretched for miles down the dusty road.

"It is all the provinces of Ireland marching against Ulster today," Maine said to Rosemary.

"But what did Ulster do to deserve this?"

"It's not what she did, it's what she has. Not only cattle and gold and slaves to plunder, but the finest prize that my mother dreams of, the Brown Bull of Cuailnge."

"A *bull?*"

"He's no ordinary bull. There's only one like him, Finn-bennach the White, which is already ours. Have you never heard the old poem?

> Great White Finnbennach
> Mountain of the herd,
> Who will possess you
> Is richer by a third.
>
> Great Brown Cuailnge
> Fury from a calf,
> Who will possess you
> Is richer by half.
>
> This no man can ever do,
> To call himself master of two."

"Well, if you can't have the two," Rosemary began.

"My mother does not know the meaning of the word 'can't.' She has gathered tribes from every part of the country to join in this Tain and while they invade Ulster and take what booty they can seize, we will capture the Brown Bull."

As it was only over the capture of a bull, Rosemary did not think the Tain a very glorious affair, but she didn't say so to Maine. He was in high spirits, whistling and singing and telling jokes as he taught her how to ride. They rode along happily together till Maeve drove up in her chariot in a cloud of noise and dust.

"End your dallying, son," she ordered, "and ride behind me. There is something I will say to the kings and chieftains that lead troops in my army."

Rosemary stifled a sigh, but Maine signalled her to follow. They rode to a hilltop where the leaders were gathering around the Queen. Rosemary waved to her brother as he drove up in Fergus's chariot. While the warrior joined the parley, Jimmy remained in the battle-car with the reins in his hands. He looked a little flushed, but well pleased with himself.

"I say the Galeoin of North Leinster must leave the march!" Maeve was shouting.

"But you still have not told me what is wrong with them," a man said reasonably.

Rosemary recognized Maine's father, Ailill, the King of Connaught.

"There is nothing wrong with them," the Queen said. "You could not find better soldiers. While the rest were clearing camp, the Galeoin were on their horses. While the rest were preparing to move, the Galeoin had ridden ten miles. Fergus leads this march but the Galeoin will arrive in

Ulster days before us. It is simple. They are too good. Too eager. They will take all the fame and plunder in this Tain, and none will go to our armies. I'll not have it!"

Ailill sighed. "Very well. We will leave them behind."

"Don't be a fool," Maeve said impatiently. "They will pillage our lands while we are gone. Kill them."

Rosemary and Jimmy looked at each other and rolled their eyes. The Queen seemed to have one solution for all problems.

"That would be an evil deed," Fergus interrupted. "You will not kill the friends of the Ulster exiles without our interference."

Maeve looked at him haughtily. "We could manage that. I have my troop of one thousand and my seven sons have theirs. It would be a simple thing."

"You overlook the fact," Fergus said in a cold voice, "that we have the seven Munster kings with us and my own army as well as the Galeoin."

Ailill raised his hand before the threats went further.

"There is no need of a battle before we reach Ulster. The Galeoin can be divided among all the armies present and their king ride with me."

"I'll agree to that," Maeve said. "You can promise him Finnabar and a corner of Ai Plain to keep him quiet. As long as their troop is not left together."

The discussion ended with that agreement and everyone dispersed to rejoin the march.

Jimmy waited till Fergus was in the chariot and seated comfortably on the bench. There was plenty of room in the battle-car. It could hold several people as well as the store of weapons, food, and cooking utensils that a fighting man

needed when he was on the move. Fergus told him to raise
the wickerwork covering to keep out the heat of the sun.
When everything was ready, Jimmy wrapped the goad in
his left hand and urged the horses till they were speeding to
the front line of the armies.

"Legs further apart," Fergus ordered. "Lean back to the
wind. You will find it is like a board behind you that gives
balance and strength. Pour your energy into the horses.
Don't slacken the reins for a moment or they will slow
down. Turn to the right to draw down the power of the sun.
That's it. If I want to challenge anyone, I will tell you to
turn to the left. It is unlucky and a sign of insult."

Jimmy followed the instructions carefully. They were
constantly repeated as he forgot one or another of the
orders. If he made a mistake too often, Fergus would give
him a hard clout over the head. Though his ears had been
ringing with these reminders all morning, he was learning
quickly, and the old warrior began to show signs that he was
pleased with him.

They overtook the first column and charged out in front
in a haze of dust and clattering. Fergus put his hand on the
boy's shoulder.

"You are doing well, son, for one not taught in the arts of
war."

"Thank you, sir," Jimmy said, without taking his eyes
from the horses.

"There is nothing wrong with your body," Fergus went
on, watching him as he handled the car, "and your mind is
good when you are made to think. Why were you not
taught to be a warrior? Are your parents low-born?"

"My father's a judge," Jimmy said offhandedly.

"A noble profession."

Fergus waited for his answer.

"Well, sir, I certainly never thought of joining the army. Actually, I haven't really thought about what I'm going to do when I'm older."

Fergus was surprised. "You are almost a man and your future has not yet been chosen? What a strange land you come from."

"And will I ever get back to it?" Jimmy wondered to himself.

But the thought was a fleeting one and soon forgotten as he came to a difficult turn in the road. He lashed out at the horses. The wild career and the spurt of speed filled him with a fierce joy.

Chapter Eight

he days passed in orderly, martial fashion as Rosemary and Jimmy fell in step with the routine of Maeve's armies. Despite aching muscles and the cold awakenings at dawn, they were soon acting like seasoned campaigners; swallowing ale and bread for breakfast, mounting horse or chariot, and keeping pace with their companions through the long, hard day.

The first overnight stop was called at Cuil Silinne by the wide blue lake of Carrcin. Late into the night the camp resounded with the protests of the Galeoin warriors as they were separated from their comrades and dispersed among the armies. Fights broke out here and there, but the Galeoin King accepted the offer of the Connaught Queen's daughter and his men could do little against it. Finnabar only laughed when she heard that she had been promised yet again.

The following morning they marched to Moin Coltna. Hunting parties broke from the companies and roamed through the brown moor, and the midday meal was a feast of roast venison. That same day, Rosemary crossed the

River Shannon in fearful silence. As the water deepened and her horse was forced to swim, she gripped the saddle desperately to keep her seat. Her fingers ached, and the freezing water seeped into her clothes, leaving her numb with cold as well as fear. Though Maine called out his encouragement, she ignored everything but the green line that wavered before her on the far side of the river. When her horse finally stumbled onto the slippery bank and threw her into the mud, she was too relieved to do anything but laugh.

The march was brought abruptly to a halt as the armies began the long and dreary business of hauling supplies, chariots, and unwilling horses across the water. By evening only half the troops had crossed. Fires burned along the east bank of the Shannon, washing the night and the river with a red glow. Around the campfires, wet clothes were dried and chilled bones warmed. The shouts and instructions and general confusion continued into the early hours of the morning till the last of the companies straggled across the river. Then began the long march across the windswept plain of Trego, the Plain of the Spears. A full day's march struggling against high winds brought them as far as the eastern-most fringe of the plain and they camped down for the night.

In the Ulster camp, Jimmy's evening training-in-arms ended. He sheathed his sword and dropped the heavy shield to the ground. As he stretched his aching arms he realized that his teacher was watching him closely.

"Again Conall?" Jimmy asked, lifting the bronze shield without complaint.

Conall Cernach smiled briefly. "That is enough for today,

James. Fergus is right. You have the will to be a warrior. It is only strength and skill that you need now."

"Not exactly the easiest things to pick up," Jimmy said ruefully.

"No," laughed Conall, "but they are useless without will. Remember that and be encouraged."

When Conall left, Jimmy put away his weapons and set out for Maeve's camp. He found his sister sitting by a fire in front of her tent.

Rosemary was lost in thought, holding a small dagger to the flames and watching the light sparkle along its edges. She looked up as Jimmy put more wood on the fire and warmed himself over it. He didn't slouch the way he used to, she noticed, and his face was tanned and hardened.

"You're changing, Jimmy," she said softly.

He smiled at her. "For the better I hope. You look good yourself."

"It's the riding. I'm getting muscles on top of muscles."

"How's the boyfriend?" he grinned. "So much for Bob, eh?"

"Bob," she repeated. "That seems to belong far away and a long time ago."

Jimmy nodded. "We've only been here a few days, but it seems much longer. I feel as if I've always been here. You don't think it's a dream anymore, do you?"

"No, and that's what worries me. Uncle Patsy must have called the police by now and maybe even telegrammed Mom and Dad."

"I didn't think about that," Jimmy said, frowning, "but there's really nothing we can do."

He poked the fire with his foot and gazed into the

burning embers. All around him were the campfires of the great army, lighting up the night sky and the dark shapes of a thousand tents. Voices could be heard calling out through the open air, and above him shone the stars and the full, round face of the moon.

"To be honest with you, Ro, I just don't worry about it. I'm enjoying this so much, I don't want to be anywhere else."

"I know what you mean," Rosemary said with a little sigh. "But that's the scary thing about it, Jim. We could lose ourselves here."

There was a rustling noise behind them as Finnabar stepped from the tent. Her hair gleamed like a golden shower around her and she wore a dress of emerald with beads of bright amber. She smiled when she saw their serious faces.

"Such long faces on the night of the moon! You are not in the right spirit, friends."

"The right spirit for what?" Rosemary said, her mood lifting at the sight of the cheerful girl.

Finnabar shook her head, bemused. "I am ever surprised, Rose, that your tribe has none of our customs. I shall have to visit you one day. But if you do not practise the rites of the Moon, my dear brother is in for a terrible disappointment," and she burst out laughing. "But quick, girl, he will be coming for you shortly and you are not even dressed! Take the blue gown I laid out for you, and silver, you must wear silver in your hair. They're in the casket by my bed. Quick, quick."

Still laughing, she pulled Rosemary away from the fire,

refusing to answer her questions, and hurried her into the tent.

When Finnabar came out again, Jimmy was already on his way back to his own camp. She ran after him, her eyes bright with excitement, and the laughter colouring her pretty face.

"James, I would request a favour of you this night. It is the feast of the full moon and we gather on the hillside to dance around the fire. I cannot go with any of my suitors. There are too many of them and they will only fight and argue over me and spoil my fun. Will you attend me?"

She saw him hesitate and she caught his arm and pleaded with him sweetly.

"Come, come sir, I am not promised to you. You will not be entangled in my marriage web. And we could dance and sing and drink wine and laugh in our freedom!"

The mischief was so alive in her face that Jimmy was close to giving in. Then he remembered the men she belonged to, and in particular, the ferocious Galeoin King.

"If there's one thing I've always avoided," he told her firmly, "it's a girl with a load of boyfriends. That's how you get your head kicked in."

Though she pouted and protested, he hurried away from her towards the Ulster camp.

"I'll probably be sorry I did that," Jimmy thought, "but then again, I'd definitely be sorry if I did the other."

In Finnabar's tent, Rosemary put on the soft woollen gown that was left out for her. She combed her long hair and bound it back with silver ornaments that matched her belt and necklace. She was admiring herself in the copper mirror, happy with the look of blue and silver against her dark hair, when she heard footsteps at the campfire.

"Rose?" Maine called.

She winked at herself in the mirror and walked regally out of the tent.

He stood waiting by the fire, resplendent in a tunic of red royal silk and a broad mantle clasped with a huge jewelled brooch. He carried no weapons and his arms and fingers sported bands of shining black jet. His fair hair fell to his shoulders and around his forehead gleamed the gold mark of his kingship.

"You look marvellous!" Rosemary said.

He touched her hair and lifted it to his lips.

"You are my outworld prize, Rose. Before you came, I thought beauty was the day and the sun. Now I know it is the gleam of night."

"Oh, I like that," Rosemary said.

He smiled and took her arm, drawing her away from the firesite and out through the camp.

The armies were settling down for their night's sleep . Fires were dying out and tent flaps closing. The sounds of people and animals grew muffled in the slow onset of silence. But something else was happening too, Rosemary realized, something different from the usual night-time routine. All around her, from the many corners of the camp, slight figures could be seen, moving stealthily in the dimness. There was whispering and the low murmur of laughter. Couples holding hands were slipping through the darkness towards a great hill on the outskirts of the companies. Rosemary stopped and withdrew her arm from Maine's.

"What is going on?" she demanded.

He heard the suspicion in her voice.

"Do you not trust me, Rose?" he asked quietly. "I have never forced a maid and never will."

"I suppose you wouldn't have to," Rosemary said wryly, but as she looked up at him, searching his face, she was sorry. His eyes were shining and there was none of the slyness she expected. Only innocence, and yes, love. She wasn't used to this. He showed his feelings simply. A weight lifted off her as she realized that no games were being played.

"You're different," she said softly. "My...people do it a different way. Not as nicely. Not half as nicely," and she smiled at him.

Together they climbed the hill where the others were gathering. A giant bonfire had been lit. In the flickering red shadows she could see the faces of nobles, warriors, and servants, all young, all merry and eager for the festival that was their own. There were musicians with great stringed instruments of bronze and gold metal that glittered in the firelight. They struck up a tune as wild as the wind, and Rosemary felt her blood tingling and her feet itching to dance. The other couples were catching hands around the fire and she joined them with Maine beside her. Before them rose the heat and brightness of the flames. Behind them, the cool air formed a circlet of velvet shade at their backs. Above glowed the arc of stars and the great silver moon in splendid fullness. The dance began. They stepped as wildly as the music, twisting and turning, intertwining, changing hands, encircling waists. Rosemary followed Maine through the dance, and he caught her up and twirled her around till she was lost in the music and his arms and the spinning stars.

The circle danced and danced, some singing as they danced. Wine was drunk and they danced again, shouting, breathless, stepping on and on. The third time the great fire fell, no one built it up again, and the dancers broke apart catching their breath and holding onto their partners.

Rosemary was leaning against Maine, her arm around his neck, still laughing and flushed from the mad gaiety.

"What are they doing?" she cried suddenly.

"Watch," Maine said, "watch them now."

They were—she couldn't believe it—they were jumping over the fire. Two by two, hands held tightly, each couple ran laughing to the flames and with a great cry leapt over them.

"They're crazy!" Rosemary said, laughing as she watched them.

Maine looked hard at her. "It is the dance of lovers. Those who jump together over the fire under the witness of the She-Moon are forged as one for all time, all ages."

Rosemary felt a twinge of shock. "I never heard of such a thing. So strange…but so beautiful."

She was thinking. He waited patiently, the question in his eyes.

Rosemary bit her lip. What if she fell in? She looked closely at the next couple who went. The girl had her dress caught up in her belt. Her legs were short and rather plump, but she made it all the same. Rosemary stared at the fire and decided it was no worse than the highjump at school. Slowly she pulled her skirts around her and tucked them into the silver chain at her waist.

"Okay," she said under her breath, and to Maine, "You realize I'll hold you personally responsible if I end up with second degree burns." But she was nervous now that she had decided to do it.

She looked up at the night sky and around the shadowy hilltop. A pagan time. A pagan rite. The ancient magic was taking hold of her. She was no longer Rosemary from modern Canada, but Rose, a Celtic girl, a woman of the stone cairns, the timeless hills, the blood passions of a warrior race. In that moment she understood an oath purged in fire, a bonding under the sight of the great moon goddess. She threw back her head as the spirit flooded through her and her face was exultant.

Maine saw the change. With a wild cry he grasped her hand, and they ran towards the fire.

Chapter Nine

he march across Ireland continued. From the Plain of Trego they journeyed into the sheltering hills of Granaird and there set up camp for the night. At dawn the next morning, Rosemary and Finnabar took up their usual place in the march, but Maine did not join them.

"He must look to his men," Finnabar said gently, when she saw Rosemary's disappointment.

"I know. Business is business," Rosemary said.

They mounted their horses and set out at a steady trot to keep pace with the companies.

"I shall tell as many jokes as he and more besides to make our day pass happily," Finnabar promised Rosemary.

"I always like being with you, Finn. You're the easiest-going person I have ever met. I don't know how you keep it up."

Finnabar sighed. "I do wonder myself sometimes. This rough wandering over the countryside with poor few belongings in boxes and baggage, is not at all to my liking. I would rather be at home in our great feasting hall of Cruachan and all my servants to look after me."

"You're too spoiled, that's your problem," Rosemary said, laughing.

"That is the truth," Finnabar agreed. "I am not suited for hardship. I miss the wonderful parties and my clothes and jewellery. Oh but it pains me to think that I will have to wear the same gown twice before this Tain is over!"

They were not on the road long before Maine rode up to them. As soon as she saw him, Rosemary knew something was wrong. His usually pleasant face was dark with anger. He nodded to her briefly before speaking to Finnabar.

"Where is the Queen?"

"She rides with Father and the Galeoin King before Maine Andoe's company."

He was about to leave, when Finnabar caught his arm.

"What is amiss, brother?"

Maine's lips were thin with rage. "My suspicions of Fergus were well founded. Have you not noticed how we travel? I must see the Queen."

As he rode away, Finnabar sat up in her saddle and looked around her.

"Ah yes," she said to Rosemary. "I do not pay attention to these things, but we are marching to the south where we should be going east." She smiled and shrugged at her companion. "Politics. That is why Maine did not join us today, so do not feel neglected. Fergus is taking us the long route, to give his kingdom time to prepare, I imagine."

"He seemed very upset," Rosemary said, looking back where Maine had ridden.

"He was against Fergus's leadership from the beginning, but Mother has her own plans. Do not concern yourself, Rose. Our armies are so great in number, Ulster cannot hope to withstand us, no matter how much time they are given."

Despite Finnabar's attempts to change the subject, Maine's discovery was soon the chief interest of the march. Small groups of horsemen sped up and down the lines from the Ulster exiles to the Connaught companies. Another parley of leaders was called by Queen Maeve. Accusations were shouted and threats made, as rumblings of complaint spread through the armies. The holiday air left the march. Gloom and suspicion dogged the men as they trudged down the long road. Even the weather played its part in the dourness that weighed upon all. The sun hid beneath a film of grey clouds and the air grew chill till the breath of the huge gathering rose like steam above them.

They halted at Cuil Sibrille for the night and the anger and tension could be felt throughout the camp. A light snow fell just as they were pitching their tents and the fires wouldn't burn on the cold, damp ground. Tempers did not improve as the companies settled down to a supper of dried meat and stale bread.

The next day Finnabar told Rosemary that four men had been ambushed and killed.

"What do you mean?" Rosemary said. Her face went white.

"He's here. Cuculann," Finnabar answered, and her voice trembled with fear and horror, "the Hound of Ulster. The Warped One. A monster who guards the borders of Cuailnge. They say he drinks the blood of his victims."

Rosemary felt sick. Things were changing too quickly from the early days of the march. The adventure was turning into a nightmare, and Jimmy rode in the front column!

It was Jimmy and Fergus who discovered the dead men. They had driven ahead of the armies to look for a ford on the River Mattock, a shallow place where the horses could cross. When they reached the ford of Ath Gabla, a grisly sight awaited them. The water of the river parted round a craggy tree that was stained and blackened. Jimmy looked up into the forked branches, and the gaping eyes of four heads stared blindly back at him. His stomach heaved.

"Do not be shy to relieve your belly," Fergus said. "You will see much worse before this raid is done with. You'll grow hardened to it soon enough."

When he had recovered, Jimmy was sent to collect the King and Queen.

"Are these our men?" Maeve demanded.

"Yes," Ailill sighed. "Four of the best in my company."

Fergus pointed to a chariot-track in the mud on the far side of the river.

"Only one man did this."

"Ulster's king?" Ailill asked.

"I think not. I believe it is Cuculann, Ulster's champion."

"We had a bad night with the cold and the snow, and now this," the Queen said angrily. "Who is the man, Fergus?"

"I will tell you. He is the Hound of Ulster, the guardian of Cuailnge. He is the greatest warrior in all Ireland; fearless in battle, invincible in skill and prowess. At five years of age he joined the boy-troop of Ulster. At seven he learned the arts of war from the witch-queen Scathach of Alba. In his eighth year he was given his weapons. He is now seventeen.''

Maeve laughed, ''Why he is just a boy, then.''

''He is known for deeds many men will never do.''

''No matter how great he is, and you Ulstermen like to exaggerate, he has only one life and we can rid him of it.''

She was no longer interested in the subject and turned in disgust from the bloodied heads.

Ailill shrugged at Fergus. ''We will stop here a while and break our fast. The men are tired and hungry from last night.''

The companies settled down for their midday meal and rumours spread through the camp like a sickness. Stories of the 'warped one' of Ulster were whispered around the fires and men clutched their weapons nervously.

In the Ulster camp, the mood was different. The warriors talked of Cuculann in words of praise and admiration. Though some showed fear as well, Jimmy noticed it was only among the younger men. Fergus and Conall Cernach called Cuculann 'dear Hound' and 'our young son', and told stories of his early days under their tutelage. They seemed highly amused that he had appeared on the Tain to worry the troops of Connaught.

When the camp broke to march, there was more confusion and shouting than usual. The captains found their troops difficult to handle, as the Connaughtmen gripped their weapons in a feverish desire to act and fight. Short words and loud curses trailed through the air, and blades were unsheathed to keep harsh discipline.

As the march moved eastwards, the terrain changed from smooth plain to stony hill. The chariot bumped and swerved over the rocky ground and Jimmy found it difficult to stay in control. After a while Fergus noticed the strain in his face.

"We will halt soon," the warrior said kindly. "Beyond these hills lies Mag Muceda, the Plain of the Pig-Keepers. We are nearing the coast and the north road to Ulster, and scouting parties will be sent out while the rest of us wait."

Jimmy revived on hearing that, and he lashed out at the horses to hurry them through the hilly pass. But as he turned a steep bend in the road, he suddenly pulled back sharply on the reins, screaming and shouting at the horses. The chariot careened madly but finally came to a halt without turning over. The road before them was blocked by a huge tree, its trunk gashed and gored with symbols. Fergus merely grunted when he saw them and once again Maeve and Ailill were sent for.

"It is a warning from Cuculann," Fergus told them. "He uses the *ogham* writing to show we are nearing his borders. He swears to travel the route of the Tain with us, killing and maiming where he has the chance."

Maeve's face reddened with fury.

"This pest must be destroyed! He's throwing the armies into a turmoil. I'll not have it!"

In a fit of rage, she drew her sword and hacked at the great tree till it lay shattered in pieces on the ground.

Word of this second encounter with the guardian of Ulster filtered through the companies till it reached Rosemary in Finnabar's train. By this time, her face was drawn and desperate.

"We've got to get out of here," she kept thinking. "We've got to get back home before something worse happens."

That night Jimmy came to see her. He laughed as he told her about Maeve's attack on the tree, and he began to praise the elusive tactics of Cuculann.

"Have you gone crazy?" Rosemary demanded suddenly. "You're talking about a murderer! He's killed four men. He's a monster, a..."

"You're listening to too many stories, Ro," Jimmy said. "Fergus says he's the greatest warrior in Ireland, and he's only seventeen. He's not murdering people. He's protecting his homeland. Remember this army is the one that's invading."

His tone infuriated her.

"Remember this army is the one that's invading," she mimicked. "How about remembering this army is the one that *we're in*! You're so busy playing cowboys and Indians, you don't even know which side you're on! This 'great hero' of yours is just as likely to kill you as anyone else. Can't you get that into your thick skull?"

Jimmy shook his head. "I don't think so. He's an Ulsterman, a friend of Fergus's, and I'm riding with the Ulster troops. Anyway, he's the type of person you have to admire no matter which side you're on. I think you're getting too upset over this. If you'd ride up front with me, instead of hiding down here with the women, and listening to horror stories..."

"Of all the stuck-up, conceited pigs!"

She glared at him, then turned her back and refused to say another word. He shrugged his shoulders and left the tent. Girls!

"There's nothing like it," Rosemary fumed, when he was

gone. "Here I am worried sick about him and he doesn't even appreciate it. I'll never speak to him again."

The next morning she was still in bad temper and she ignored Finnabar's attempts to draw her into conversation. But as the day wore on, she began to feel less indignant and to regret the argument. She didn't like fighting with Jimmy. She had just decided that she would find him at the next halt and apologize, when Maine rode up to her with a terrible look on his face.

"I do not like to be a bearer of ill news, Rose, but your brother is missing from the side of Fergus."

Chapter Ten

hen the camp set out that morning from Mag Muceda, Jimmy had forgotten his argument with Rosemary. The road from the plain was rutted and muddy, and Jimmy had to keep stopping to push the chariot. When they reached solid ground, Fergus leaned over the edge of the battle-car.

"We are in need of cleaning, charioteer. The earth on the wheels is slowing us down."

"Take a horse, Fergus," Jimmy said. "I saw a lake not far back. I'll take it there and give it a wash."

Fergus smiled at the boy's confident air.

"You can manage to drive alone and catch up with me?"

"Of course, sir."

Jimmy turned the chariot and headed back against the coming tide of the army. When he came to the lake, he freed the horses to graze and pulled the car down to the water. He scraped, scoured and washed, puffing with the effort till his face was flushed and hot.

"You are doing a fine job there," someone said.

Jimmy looked up to see a young man leaning against a tree and watching him with interest. A great sword hung at his side and he dangled a spear in his hand.

"It's the least I can do," Jimmy said, straightening his back, "for the honour of driving it."

"Well said."

The stranger smiled. He wasn't very tall but he was broad and stocky. The muscles of his arms and legs were tight and knotted, showing great power and strength. He had long yellow hair tied back from his bare face, and his eyes were bright and friendly.

"It would be easier if you held the chariot up," he suggested.

Jimmy's face reddened. He didn't like the young warriors on the march. They were too cocky and conceited, and they were always making fun of his lack of skill.

"If you think that's such a great idea, why don't you do it yourself?" he said shortly.

The stranger looked amused. He walked over to the chariot and bending down, lifted it out of the water till it was resting on his shoulders and back. Without the slightest show of strain, he said, "Here you go, my friend. I'll hold it till you're finished."

Jimmy gaped, his resentment quickly turning to admiration. Without a word, he set about scraping and cleaning the undersides of the car. When the work was done and the chariot stood fresh and gleaming, Jimmy put out his hand.

"Thanks. I couldn't have done it so well or so quickly without your help."

The stranger shrugged as they shook hands.

"It was nothing… Your hands have new marks on them. You have not been a charioteer long?"

"Just a week, actually, but I'm learning fast. Fergus has stopped bashing my head so I must be getting better."

At the mention of Fergus, the young man burst out laughing.

"So you ride with my old friend?"

"What's so funny about that? He's the best as far as I'm concerned."

"Oh I agree with you. But you do not look like an Ulsterman."

"I'm not, but I'm not a Connaughtman either."

"I'm glad to hear that. What's your name and where do you come from?"

"James. From Canada."

"James. What a peculiar name. And from where? Canada?" He drew the last word out, putting an accent on the end of it. "That must be far away. I've never heard tell of it."

"It's off to the west," Jimmy said vaguely. "What's your name? You're an Ulsterman aren't you?"

"Yes. I am Cuculann of Ulster."

Jimmy's mouth fell open and he stared at the man in confusion.

"I take it you've heard of me," Cuculann said easily.

Though his legs were shaking, Jimmy reached for his sword. Cuculann was quicker and he grabbed Jimmy's arm before he could touch the scabbard and threw him to the ground. They rolled in the grass, each trying to get a grip on the other. They tumbled into the lake, spluttering and cursing as the water poured over them. As Jimmy puffed and grappled, it occurred to him that this was hardly the glorious combat he had been trained for. It was more like a tussle with his school friends. Despite the danger and his own fear, the thought made him laugh out loud. Cuculann stopped in surprise, then laughed himself. He jumped up and hauled Jimmy out of the water. They whooped and laughed, slapping their thighs and shaking the mud off their feet.

"You are hardly a seasoned warrior, my friend," Cuculann said, still laughing.

"Again, just for a week," Jimmy said with a grin. "Fergus would have a fit if he saw the results of his work."

"I think not," Cuculann said seriously. "I did not intend to kill you, but you had no way of knowing that, and yet you showed no fear. That is the mark of a fighting man and you have it."

"Somehow you don't strike me as an enemy, I guess."

"Then we will be friends," said the warrior, putting his hand on Jimmy's shoulder.

Even as he spoke, Cuculann's face changed and his eyes clouded with a sudden bitterness.

"What's wrong?"

"It's well, I'm thinking, to have a friend," Cuculann said heavily. "Someone who doesn't want to kill me."

"Are you all alone?"

"My charioteer Laeg was killed by four men at the ford of Ath Gabla. They attacked him when he was bathing and he had little chance to defend himself. I am now alone in my fight against this great army."

Jimmy looked at him with sympathy and then a thought struck him.

"I'll stay with you!" he cried, and the sudden brightening of Cuculann's face confirmed it. "Fergus did well enough without me before I came. It's not right that you have to battle alone against these odds, no matter who you are."

But he felt guilty as soon as he thought of Fergus. The old soldier had treated him like a son.

"I know what I'll do," he said. "Fergus spoke well of you and you call him your friend. I'll take the chariot back to him—they should be breaking for a meal about now—and I'll ask him if I can join you."

"Good idea, James of Canada," Cuculann said, slapping him on the back and looking very happy. "Fergus won't begrudge me his charioteer. He knows I am in need of company on this Tain. I will wait for you here."

Jimmy drove back to Fergus who roared laughing when he heard the plea.

"It is not any man who can become the friend of the Great Hound. I am amazed your head is still attached to your body. But then," he added, looking at Jimmy's eager face, "there is something about you that both Cuculann and I can see. You'll do him good, I think, and he you. Be off, then, before it is too late for you to escape. Take a horse and speak to no one if you can help it. Tell Cuculann that six await him at the ford of Ath meic Garach, an ambush once again and an unfair fight at that."

Hearing this warning, Jimmy was in a hurry to return to his new friend. As he mounted his horse, Fergus looked up at him with fatherly pride and affection.

"Remember all I have taught you, James. That Cuculann should take you to his heart is already a sign I have done well with you. We will meet again."

"Thank you for everything, sir."

In his haste to leave the camp and to escape without

notice, Jimmy forgot about his sister. He happily rode out, leaving the camp of Maeve and the company of Fergus, to join with a warrior of his own age—a friend who needed him.

Chapter Eleven

'd give anything for a piece of toast right now," Jimmy said, as he sat on the ground to have his breakfast.

He had watched hungrily as Cuculann fried their catch of fish over the fire.

"Toast?" said Cuculann.

"It's hard to explain when you don't know what a toaster is," the boy replied, "but if I can find a long stick," and he rummaged through the kindling, "I'll just put a piece of bread on the end of it—too bad your bread's so hard, and no butter—but here goes nothing."

He held the unleavened bread over the fire until it was generally brown and also a bit black, then handed it to Cuculann.

"Hmm. Burnt bread," Cuculann said, making a face as he chewed it. "What strange habits you have. I cannot say I like it."

Jimmy laughed and toasted himself a piece. "With a bit of cheese melted onto it, it'll be great."

When they were finished eating, Jimmy yoked the horses to the chariot as Cuculann gathered his weapons and cleared the campsite.

"We must away to our work, charioteer," Cuculann said. "I want you to learn to handle *my* chariot, now. No man is alike in how he fights or rides, and I will need you to know my ways."

For most of the day, Jimmy practised driving the battle-car under his friend's command. As dusk crept over the hillsides, they set out eastward to find the armies. The chariot was pulled by Cuculann's great steeds as lightly as a leaf carried on the wind, and Jimmy felt his tiredness wash away in the cool rushing of the air. They rode for miles through the silence of the night and didn't stop till dawn paled over the hushed, damp fields. As they came in sight of the armies, Jimmy halted on a hilltop. Below them, the road was black with the moving columns of men, their weapons flashing in the early sunlight. From where he stood, Jimmy could see the blue glimmer of the sea like a thin line on the horizon.

"I see a giantess," Cuculann said. "Red hair and a yellow cloak. She carries her shield like a man and grips a stinging sword above her head in rage."

Jimmy squinted into the sun.

"You've got great eyesight to go along with everything else, Cucuc. I know you're talking about Maeve but I can't see her."

"Well then," Cuculann said with a mischievous grin, "you can't see the pet squirrel that sits on her shoulder."

He leaned into the chariot and pulled out a slingshot and

a small, round pebble. Closing one eye and holding the sling high, he let the stone fly. A few seconds later he began to laugh.

Jimmy whooped, "I bet she's cursing blue murder!"

They laughed and howled till their sides ached. Then Cuculann looked again at the army.

"I see chariots breaking from the lines. They hope to catch us if we are following but we shall catch them instead. Northwards, James, to meet them at the ford. Let us test our new partnership!"

They sped down the hill in the direction the Connaught cars had taken. Jimmy shivered with excitement but he kept his eyes on the horses and waited for Cuculann's orders. When they reached the ford, they found many chariots waiting for them.

"Into the midst of them!" Cuculann cried.

There was no time for hesitation or panic. Jimmy drove furiously into the line of chariots. The roar of breaking wood and screaming horses deafened him. Earth and debris flew in the air and the war cries of Cuculann howled through his brain. He pulled the reins and spun the car around as they cleared the first onslaught. Cuculann began casting spears to bring down the enemy charioteers till the Connaught cars crashed and broke against each other.

"To the left, Jim!" he cried, as a hail of spears and javelins fell around them.

Jimmy brought the chariot round to face the remaining foe. Terror gorged in his throat as men ran at him with their swords held high.

"Move!" Cuculann roared, and he jumped out onto the chariot pole.

Jimmy drove into the men as Cuculann swung his sword in a wide arc to clear their path. They broke through the attack to face the chariots that had reformed in the confusion. Straining to the utmost, Jimmy turned and twisted the car, darting in and out and around the enemy while Cuculann hacked and slew.

Finally there was silence.

Chariots lay upturned, their wheels spinning, their shafts smashed and broken. Men lay dead, trampled by their horses, with spears in their sides and great gashes across their bodies. Maddened, their flanks crimson, the horses fled from the scene. Exhaustion and relief flooded over Jimmy and he leaned weakly against the chariot.

"A good day's work, charioteer," Cuculann said with a satisfied grimace.

He began cutting off heads, then stopped and muttered, "No time for trophies," and he collected his spears instead, pulling the unbroken ones from the bodies of the slain. As he wiped his weapons clean on the grass, he looked up at Jimmy's worn face.

"We're not finished yet, Jim. Come here and I'll show you my plan."

Jimmy groaned inwardly, but he hunched down beside the warrior who was marking the ground with his dagger.

"We are here. Ath Carpat. And here's the river that runs before us to the sea. The River Nith. The armies will go south of the rivermouth through the marshes of Saili Imdorchi and wait for low tide. It's the only way they could go with their huge numbers and all their provisions. Then they'll cross the Broad Ford to Cuailnge.

"Now...we can't attack from here or there, because it's

too open and we'd be overwhelmed by sheer numbers. We'll go on ahead and cross the Broad Ford before them. Can you swim? Good. There's a spot in the Cuailnge hills, Sliab Cuinciu, the Stony Mountain, where we can camp and take a long rest till they arrive. How does that sound?"

Jimmy was cheered by the idea of a long rest somewhere in the near future.

"Sounds great to me," he said.

They drove swiftly from Ath Carpat and soon caught up with the slow advance of the armies. Keeping to the shelter of hill and wood, they shadowed the Connaught forces, till the companies broke for their meal. Then Jimmy and Cuculann circled around the camp and on to the Broad Ford that lay before the peninsula of Cuailnge.

To Jimmy, the wide ford looked more like a lake or a bay and he balked at the idea of swimming across it. It was a full day since he had slept and every part of his body ached with weariness.

"Courage, Jim," Cuculann said behind him. "This is the last hurdle and then we rest."

The cold dark water shocked Jimmy awake and he plunged into the depths before he lost his nerve altogether. The muscles of his arms and legs ached with pain as he thrashed out wildly in the hopes of shortening the ordeal, but it seemed like hours before he caught even a glimpse of the land ahead. His eyes stung with the salt of the sea-water, his stomach was sick with it, but still he fought to keep himself afloat and moving. Behind him swam Cuculann dragging horses and chariot. How many times had the warrior pulled him up as he slipped beneath the surface? At last he was crawling onto the sandy shore of Cuailnge and he lay there with his eyes closed. After a time he felt Cuculann lift him into the chariot, but it wasn't till the warrior picked up the reins that he roused himself.

"Oh no you don't," Jimmy said, pulling himself up shakily. "I'm the charioteer... where's that mountain?"

When they reached Sliab Cuinciu, a high stony ridge bedraggled with old trees and bushes, Jimmy drew up the chariot and collapsed. Cuculann moved around him quietly, building a fire and freeing the horses to graze. As he placed a blanket over Jimmy, he looked down a moment and spoke softly.

"You did much more than I thought you capable of, James. And you are worth more to me in friendship than you will ever know. I thank the god who sent you to me on this Tain."

Chapter Twelve

aeve's armies moved slowly through the wet lands that bordered the River Nith. Cuculann's harassment was the daily talk of the march, but Rosemary no longer cared. She rode in a daze of shock and grief. There was no word or sign of Jimmy. Maine went to ask questions in the Ulster camp, but he was met with blank stares and open hostility. When he approached Fergus, the old warrior greeted him coldly.

"Have you come again, son of Maeve, to argue my leadership of this march?"

Maine returned to Rosemary with empty words, but she refused to accept that her brother was dead. As time passed, she began to think more clearly. There was no use in crying and moping. If Jimmy were in trouble she would have to do something. Her only hope was to find the Druid and make him help them. She wanted to tell Maine and Finnabar her plan, but decided against it. It would not be easy to leave Maeve's camp. Deserters were killed without question. She would have to escape and the fewer who knew about it the better. But how would she find the Druid?

That night, with only a vague notion of what she sought, Rosemary visited the servants' camp. Hooded by her mantle, she wandered through the rough camp asking here and there about the Druids and their habits. While some people shook their heads and turned away as if they couldn't speak of such things, others brought her into their dark tents to tell long tales of superstition and magic. After hours of fruitless searching and talk, a young woman finally told her the truth of the matter.

"The Druithin are a priesthood of secrecy. No one really knows what they do or where they go."

Bitter with disappointment, Rosemary stumbled from the camp and made her way across the plain. As she neared her own site, she came upon an old manservant huddled over a dying fire. His thin shoulders were shaking in the chill of the night air. When she saw that he was alone and far from the other camps, Rosemary forgot her own misery. She collected bits of wood and dried branches and fed his campfire till it rose high and warm. The old man tucked his feet under him, but said nothing, and she turned to leave.

"You've been asking questions."

His voice crackled like the burning wood and she wasn't sure if he had spoken. She hesitated and he looked up at her. His face was old and scarred like a dried river bed. His eyes were dark and watery.

"I'm looking for someone," she said, hardly daring to believe that he could help her.

He nodded and looked back to the fire.

"The Hound of the Sea," he said.

Her heart sank. More stories.

"It is the Murricu you seek, is it not?"

She caught her breath. Wasn't that the name Peter had used? Peadar Murricu?

"Yes. Yes," she said eagerly. "That's who I'm looking for. Do you know where he is?"

"Aye. He said you and another would come looking for him. He left word with me, but you never came."

"I didn't think…"

The old man spat into the fire and it hissed back at him.

"Nobody thinks around here," he said indifferently.

Rosemary looked at him uneasily. She and Jimmy had only made a half-hearted search for the Druid. She realized now that they had not really wanted to find him.

"Am I too late?" she asked anxiously.

"You may be and you may not be," he answered. "The message is this. 'Seek for others and ye shall find. Seek for self and ye be blind.'"

"A riddle?" Rosemary said desperately. "But what does it mean?"

"I just hold and give messages, girl. That is all I am called to do. You must find the meaning yourself. Good night."

With that the old man closed his eyes as if she had already left. Rosemary fought back her tears. It was a cruel joke, an unfair game, to come this close and not understand.

"Did you bring the wood?" the old man suddenly asked.

He had opened one eye and was staring at the loud fire as if he had just seen it.

"Yes."

"Then I am obliged to you," but he spoke as if it made no difference to him. "Go to the wood of Es Ruaid, to the Harper of Cain Bile. It is he who holds the answers and deems the worth of seekers."

"Oh, thank you, thank you, I appreciate your help, believe me. Is there anything else I can do for you?"

But once again his eyes were closed, dismissing her with finality. She murmured her farewells and hurried back to the camp. Rushing breathlessly into her tent, she grabbed Finnabar's arm.

"Where's Es Ruaid?"

"Why do you…"

"Never mind, Finn, where is it?" she demanded.

Finnabar stared at her as if she had gone mad.

"It is a wood by the mouth of the river," she answered in a puzzled voice.

"Is there a man living there? A harper or something?"

"Why—how did you know? Yes, I've heard it said that a powerful Druid haunts those woods, the sweet-mouthed Harper of Cain Bile. But no one has seen him. No one goes there. It's an enchanted and unlucky place. You're not thinking…?"

"No, of course not," Rosemary said hurriedly. "I heard some children talking about it. You know, scary stories." She laughed nervously. "They upset me a bit."

"Ah you poor girl. You did frighten me when you came in so fiercely. I know you have not been yourself since… but you are looking much improved now, I am glad to say." Finnabar's voice was kind and concerned. "Will you sleep tonight, do you think?"

"I'm sure I will," Rosemary said, feeling a little guilty. "As a matter of fact, I'm going to bed right now. How about you?"

"I shall," Finnabar said. "I am so tired. Mother kept me for hours tonight. I combed and combed her hair and still she was angry and unappeasable."

Finnabar went on about the Queen and the progress of the march till Rosemary was nearly frantic. At last the girl undressed and lay down to sleep. Rosemary waited till her breaths grew slow and even.

"Finn?" she whispered.

"Finnabar?" she said, more loudly.

When the girl didn't stir, Rosemary dressed carefully and slipped from the tent. It was a good night for travelling. The sky was clear and the moon shone like a lantern. She crept from the camp and made her way down to the river. How long a journey she faced was uncertain, but she couldn't take her horse for fear of rousing the sentries. The black rush of the river was her only companion, as she trudged for hours through bush and marshland. Her feet grew sore and blistered, but her spirits were high and she sang to herself as she walked. Now that she was doing something she felt there was hope for herself and her brother.

"Oh Jimmy, please be alive," she prayed to the sky.

The stars winked back their encouragement and she was happier than she had been in days. At last she could see the still glitter of the sea before her and she knew she was nearing the mouth of the river. But when she came to the end of her journey, she stared in horror.

Es Ruaid was not a wood but a great ancient forest. Where the line of trees began, even the moonlight was shut out, and it was like entering a dark and baneful tomb. The wind whined above her, trapped in the tangled branches. The air was thick with the night perfume of whispering leaves. The ground was damp and mossy, and gnarled with roots like the back of an old man's hand. Rosemary stepped uneasily, listening to the sounds of the forest, afraid to look around her. She imagined dark shapes moving through the underbrush, keeping pace with her movements.

"There is nothing here. There is nothing following me," she kept repeating.

Then she heard it distinctly. A soft muffled sound, over to her left. She stopped and peered through the dimness. Something moved behind the tree trunk, she was sure of it. She dug her nails into her palms and walked faster. There it was again, behind her now. Mute whispers. And padded footfall. She couldn't bear it any longer. She screamed and started to run. The trees closed in around her, the branches clutching at her hair and arms, scratching her face.

"Peter!" she cried in terror. "Murricu! You told me to come here. Where are you?"

Her cry rang through the forest and the wind in the trees tossed it back, a wild mockery of her fear. Rosemary fell to the ground and hid her face in her arms. Then silence. The wind stopped. The trees stood still. Quiet settled over her and she lay without moving. Then a new sound came to her, one that didn't belong to the malevolent forest. She raised her head to listen. A voice was singing, far away; high, sweet notes trailing through the darkness. She saw a light glowing in the trees, bobbing gently like a will-o-the-wisp. It was moving toward her and as it drew closer so too did the voice. Then she saw the shining singer. Though he appeared to be young, his hair was completely white, flow-ing over his shoulders like a stream. He walked barefoot, and the loose robes that fell to his feet were also white as was the wooden staff he leaned upon. The light that Rosemary had seen was all around him, issuing from his body like silvery breath. He was still singing as he approached her, and his voice was so beautiful that it made her want to laugh and cry at the same time. It was a song as sharp and unearthly as the pure air of a mountain peak. He stopped singing when he saw her and stooped down to lift her to her feet.

"Are you all right, child?" he asked and his voice was rich and warm.

She looked into his face. Serenity shone in his features, and in his eyes as still and blue as the summer sea. He was so radiant it took her a few moments to realize that she recognized him, and yet even that shock could not break the peace he instilled in her.

"Are you Peter?" she asked.

His smile was gentle but she saw a shadow flicker across his face.

"I am and I am not," he said. "I am the Harper of Cain Bile. I am part of he whom you know and that part which he seeks."

"Is he here?" Rosemary asked eagerly.

There was a sadness in the Harper's eyes.

"He came seeking, but he came blindly and found not."

"He's gone, then?" she whispered. "I'm too late?"

Her disappointment was like a stab of pain and she couldn't stop herself from crying, "I needed him. He's the only one who can help us."

"Child, there is always someone who can help," the Harper said, and he put his arm around her shoulder and led her through the forest.

It was like a dream to walk beside him. The light which shone from him brightened everything like a slow, seeping fire. There was music in the air around him, and a sense of joy and contentment which was like a cloud you could almost touch. She felt the tiredness and despair leave her, and she would have been happy to walk with him forever.

They broke from the trees into a small, moonlit clearing. The grass shone like silk and the place seemed warm and friendly after the dark forest that crouched at its edge. In the glade stood a small stone dwelling shaped like a beehive. As she stooped to enter, Rosemary saw it was empty but for a smooth marble table in the centre of the floor. The table was flooded with moonlight from an opening in the roof above it.

"Is this your home?" Rosemary asked, surprised. There was a hollow and unused feeling to the place.

The Harper smiled. "The forest is my home. The leafy branches are my shelter, the soft earth, my floor, and the roots of the great oak tree, my bier. This is a house of vision, where answers can be found."

"You mean I can ask where my brother is?" Rosemary cried. "And Peter? You see, Jimmy has disappeared and..."

The Harper gently placed his fingers on her lips.

"Hush, child, there is no need to tell me. I know what you seek. And I know it is for another and not yourself. That is why the Song led me to you and why it will answer. Sit there upon the floor and your time will come to question."

Rosemary did as she was told and watched in silence as

the Harper lay himself upon the marble table. He had been a source of great light before, but now as he lay beneath the circle of the moon, his brilliance increased a hundredfold till it burst around him like a fabulous silver flower. He began to sing. It was not a human voice, but more like the delicate rippling of harp strings. The music rose and fell in filigrees of sound that intertwined in the air. She could see the tune weaving itself in silver light and threading a shining web around her. She was made the centre of the sparkling pattern, and she knew it was time to speak.

"I am looking for my brother," she said simply. Her voice echoed a moment and was absorbed into the web. "I don't know if he is alive or dead. I am looking for Peadar Murricu, the Druid who brought us here. I want to ask him to help us."

She bowed her head as she finished, and the silver light played its sweet music around her. She began to feel drowsy and felt herself slipping into unconsciousness. There was a movement near her and half asleep she saw the Harper rising from the stone. He was speaking to her and it took all her will and effort to listen.

"I see him. Your brother lives. I see a dark shadow over him, and you also. Death is near. I see the Murricu and he has caught sight of me. His knowledge grows, for even as I sent him the vision of your peril, he moves to help, and in so doing, he draws closer to me."

The Harper leaned over Rosemary but try as she would, her eyes could not stay open and she was already drifting into sleep. He touched her forehead and his hand was cool and seemed to cleanse her mind of thought.

"Have courage, child of another world. There is hardship ahead, but you have the strength to face it."

They were the last words that Rosemary heard before she fell into a deep, deep sleep.

Chapter Thirteen

t was a warm, golden morning and Jimmy and Cuculann sat at their ease over a wooden playing board. They had cleared a campsite on the stony ridge of Sliab Cuinciu and were using blocks of stone for table and chairs. Jimmy concentrated for a while on the bronze pieces shaped like cattle and human figures. Then he made his move.

"You can't put that man there," Cuculann said, exasperated. "He's a satirist. He doesn't fight. He can help your warrior-piece move two paces or he can knock down my man there, *if*," and he grinned, "you make up a good poem."

Jimmy wrinkled his forehead. That was right. A satirist could advance a warrior double the usual move or else shame one of Cuculann's into retreat, but it didn't move by itself.

"I was thinking of it as a pawn," said Jimmy.

"This is not the game you keep referring to," Cuculann said with a laugh. "What do you call it? Chess? This is *fidchell*, so keep your mind on it. I've only beaten you four times in a row."

The younger boy sighed, "It doesn't make things any easier when you drag poetry into it. English was never my best subject." He thought a moment, then smothered a chuckle and spoke in a solemn tone—

"Move along you dirty blighter,
What I cannot say in prose
A poem will get you fighter
Though I'd rather punch your nose."

Cuculann snorted and fell off his seat roaring with laughter.

"A curse! You have to finish with a curse!"

"Geronimo!" Jimmy yelled in excitement. "Off with your head, ban the bomb, and up the flag!"

Cuculann howled till the tears streamed down his face, and they both shrieked and hooted.

"All right my boy," Cuculann said, getting back on his seat and wiping his eyes, "I'll let you have it. But by the gods, my teacher Amargin would have a fit if he heard that. Poetry you call it?"

"It's all in the eye of the beholder," Jimmy said modestly.

Cuculann placed his warrior-piece back in his own territory and concentrated on his next move. Jimmy, on the other hand, had to decide if he should stay on the defensive, or send his king into the empty space and declare a raid. If he lost the raid, though, he would have to yield a large section of his boardspace, or worse, his gold piece. He had plenty of time to work it out as Cuculann didn't make his moves quickly.

"What do they teach you in your country, Jim, if you do not learn hunting and poetry and the skills of war?"

"My father says they teach us nothing at all, but we learn things like reading and writing, math, physics, geography…"

"Hmm. Some of these words are strange to me. I can write the ogham on stone and wood, and read the tracks of armies and the flight of birds. I know the positions of the stars and the properties of plants and herbs…What is 'geography'?"

"Boring, as far as I'm concerned. I dunno. Learning where places are, how rivers flow, why the land is flat or mountainous. Stuff like that."

Cuculann looked perplexed.

"Why would anyone teach you that? Don't you learn such things from your own eyes and from your wanderings? I see the river running to the sea. The people who live by it tell me it has run thus for ten generations upon ten generations. Therefore, I know that it was the river which tore the great gap through the mountains. I know where places are and what they are like by going there myself."

"What about places you'll never get to?"

"Why would I want to know about them if I'll never go there?"

"For general knowledge, I guess."

Cuculann laughed, "What kind of knowledge is that, something you'll never use? Better to spend your time learning things you need to know."

"I couldn't agree with you more, but that's the way it goes in school."

"What a ridiculous picture it makes," the warrior mused.

"A land of people with knowledge they don't need or use. I can't imagine why it hasn't been conquered by now."

"Oh, most of my world is the same way," Jimmy said.

In the silence that followed, he realized he had said too much.

"You are not of this world then," Cuculann said.

"No. I'm pretty sure I'm not."

Jimmy waited anxiously to see how he would take this, but the warrior only shrugged.

"I thought as much."

"Doesn't it bother you that I can pop in from nowhere like that?"

"Why should it? There are mortals and there are gods, and though we don't live in the same place we live in the same time. Often the two worlds touch."

"There must be more than two worlds," Jimmy pointed out, "because I'm not a god, that's for sure. I'd be more inclined to think you and your people are."

Cuculann laughed, "No, James, I and my people will die and the gods do not. I will tell you something of the mixing of my world with the gods. You know of the Sidhe? You must call your gods something else. The Sidhe are the gods of Ireland. They know us well and we know something of them. They are a warrior race like ourselves, but they are immortal and have great powers." He leaned towards Jimmy and his eyes shone with a strange light, "You have said, friend, that I fight unlike any other man you have seen. There is a reason for that. I am more than a man, though still mortal. I am the son of Lug mac Ethenn, the God with the Spear. The blood of the Sidhe mingles with my mother's blood in me."

Jimmy stared back at him, wondering if this were super-stition or if it could be true. Then he remembered Cucu-lann's amazing abilities. These were things that couldn't happen in his own world but they were certainly real in this one. He was about to ask more questions, when they heard scrambling noises on the ridge. Jimmy ran to look and called back to the warrior.

"One man only, heading this way!"

"Describe him to me," Cuculann said.

"A tall man, wearing a brown cloak. He has funny-looking shoes and he's carrying a branch, I think, in his left hand."

"That's a hazel wand, stripped bare. The shoes, cloak and branch are the signs of a herald. It is Mac Roth of Connaught, I'll warrant. You can sit and relax, Jim."

But the boy remained standing till the messenger ran up to them.

"Whose servant are you?" he demanded of Jimmy.

"I am the charioteer of this man," Jimmy replied, nod-ding to Cuculann.

"And whose servant are you?" the herald asked Cuculann who was still bent over the game.

"I stand with Conchobor mac Nessa, King of Ulster."

"Then you are the man I seek. I bear a message from Ailill, King of Connaught. He offers you a part of Ai Plain as great as Murtheimne your own land, twenty bondsmaids, his finest chariot, and compensation for any cattle you may have lost. In return for this you will fight for Connaught."

Cuculann moved his king-piece and to Jimmy's chagrin declared a raid.

"I would not betray my blood for money," he said mildly. "You forget I am Conchobor's nephew."

"That is your answer?"

Cuculann motioned to Jimmy to sit down and turned to the herald with a friendly look.

"It has been a hard three days in Cuailnge, Mac Roth, for the armies of Maeve and Ailill."

"Aye," said Mac Roth, answering the easy tone. "It has."

"They were unable to cross the River Cronn, I heard."

The herald nodded. "On the first day of our march in Cuailnge, the river rose against us and a hundred and twenty-four were drowned."

The warrior smiled. "The river is on my land and answers to my call. Tell your Queen that. She has a temper, has she not?"

Mac Roth grinned. "She tore up the ground to insult Ulster, leaving a great gaping wound from the Cronn to Glenn Dailimda."

"She will pay for that," Cuculann said softly. "They were unable to cross the River Colptha also, I think."

The messenger nodded again.

"On the second day of our march, the River Colptha rose and drowned a hundred. Two hundred and twenty-four men died before the armies reached the Plain of Conaille."

Jimmy was listening to the conversation in astonishment but he said nothing as Cuculann spoke again in a stern voice.

"Tell Maeve and Ailill that I am my land and the land is me. But now that they have settled on Conaille Plain I shall begin to act with my own arms and legs."

Hearing these words, Mac Roth remembered his duty.

"Is there nothing that will stop you from this slaughtering?"

"There is. I will fight in single combat by the ford. While this is taking place, your armies are to take no more cattle from Cuailnge and I will not harass by night or day."

When the herald left, Cuculann explained to Jimmy, "The single combat is the only way I can keep them from further plundering."

But Jimmy's mind was racing with the words Cuculann had exchanged with Mac Roth.

"Cucuc, are you even more powerful than I thought? Is that why we've been doing nothing for the past three days? Were you using magic?"

Cuculann looked puzzled, then burst out laughing.

"The only magic there, Jim, was the stupidity of Mac Roth's brain. I was only guessing and he told me everything I wanted to know."

"But the rivers," Jimmy insisted. "Did you call up the rivers?"

The warrior's laughs grew louder. "What was your word for it? Geography? Those two rivers always flood at this time of year."

Jimmy laughed loudly and Cuculann smirked.

"Now that idiot will go back and tell the camp I have the powers of a Druid. They will be twice as frightened of me."

"Brilliant. Absolutely brilliant!" Jimmy cried.

Cuculann tried to look modest. "It's all part of the wiles that Sencha the Sage taught me."

The warrior sighed. "So now we know the journey that the army has taken in Cuailnge and judging by Mac Roth's words their only hardship was the rivers. I was right not to follow them. The men of Ulster have not yet arisen. We are still alone against this huge force."

"Why Cucuc? Why is Ulster so slow to join you? I know myself that Fergus sent warnings to them when he detoured the march."

"It has to do with what we were talking about before," Cuculann said. "The mixing of the worlds, the visits of the Sidhe to this world. Sometimes such visits are not for the best. But it is a long tale, Jim, and we cannot spend our day in idleness. We must leave here and camp on the Hill of Ochaine which overlooks Conaille Plain. We will be in sight of the armies, there, and can take up our duties once more."

Chapter Fourteen

immy and Cuculann journeyed westwards to the Hill of Ochaine and set up their camp that afternoon.

"I will take the horses, Jim," Cuculann said, when the fire had been built up. "I think it is certainly your turn to cook a meal."

Jimmy looked embarrassed and Cuculann raised his eyebrows.

"Do not tell me you can't cook! You are not even taught *that* in your world?"

"Only the girls," Jimmy admitted.

Cuculann was surprised.

"But surely you do not have women with you all the time? Do the men prefer to depend on women rather than learn this skill?"

Jimmy felt very uncomfortable as he tried to think of an answer, and in the end he could only shrug.

"Beats me. I just never thought about it," he said lamely.

Cuculann gave an exaggerated sigh. "I shall have to teach you this as well. First, the water on the fire. Toss in herbs for flavour. Here, wash these and cut them into small pieces."

"Nettles?!"

"The finest plant for a hearty soup. Throw them in when you are finished."

Cuculann took a bag of flour from the chariot and mixed it with water in a wooden bowl. Then he rolled the dough into soft round balls.

"Dumplings, my young charioteer," he said. "Drop them in the pot when it boils. I'll snare us a fat rabbit and we shall have a feast."

After their meal they lay back to enjoy the warmth of the late afternoon. They talked lazily about war, the rules of combat, chariot-racing and the upkeep of weapons. In the distance, the campfires of Maeve's armies burned on the plain like a bush fire.

"Look over there," Jimmy said, squinting at a black figure moving towards them.

"My first challenger," Cuculann said. "They have accepted the terms of single combat."

Jimmy shuddered as the man drew nearer and stood at the foot of the hill. He was more like a great, hairy beast than a man, an ape-like bear. Where his body wasn't covered with its own black hair or the skins of animals, it was spattered with crimson and blue paint. As he began to climb the hill, Cuculann jumped up.

"Not at my camp!" he roared down. "The foot of the hill, you dolt!"

The beast-man shook his fist menacingly and trudged off to the appointed spot. Cuculann turned to Jimmy with a look of disgust on his face.

"Cur mac Dalath, a savage," he said with a sniff. "Maeve

has sent him to get him out of her sight. He eats raw meat and stinks like a foul pit." Cuculann belched loudly. "I'll work off my meal anyway."

"Are you never afraid?" Jimmy asked, not bothering to hide his admiration.

"What is there to fear? Pain? I have suffered a thousand wounds. There is no part of my body that has not been gashed, gored, or broken. Death? I laugh at death. It can only come once to me and then it is over. Shame or dishonour? I cannot know these as long as I don't fear pain or death."

Cuculann stood proud and shining. His eyes were bright with youthful courage and humour. Jimmy handed him his weapons with new formality.

"I will display a few feats for you, friend, before the combat begins. I will show you what I was taught when I was a child."

With a great thrust he stood three spears butt-end in the ground. Taking a deep breath, he leapt high into the air and landed on the points, dancing there without a drop of blood appearing on his feet. Jimmy watched in wonder and clapped vigorously when he was finished. Cuculann bowed.

"That was the hero's coil on the spikes of spears. It teaches agility and control of pain."

He threw a spear ahead of him and out-racing it, jumped upon the shaft and rode it to the ground.

"Bravo!" Jimmy cried.

Cuculann danced on the hot coals of the fire, laughing at Jimmy's concern. He leapt across the hill and back again, as if he were flying. In a burst of enthusiasm, he tore the wheel from the chariot and threw the huge weight into the air, catching it as it twirled heavily to the ground. His face was flushed and his eyes shone. He let out a great roar and thumped his admirer on the back.

"I am ready now. My blood runs hot in my body and demands release."

Resplendent in his rage, Cuculann rushed to attack the beast-man. But the man didn't move to defend himself and before Jimmy could run to see what was going on, Cuculann was back at the campsite fuming and spluttering.

"That fool! That hairy idiot! He won't fight me. He called me a beardless boy. What will I do? This could shame me forever!"

If Cuculann hadn't been so upset, Jimmy would have laughed. Instead he ran to the fire and pulled out a piece of charred wood. In an instant he had blackened the warrior's chin and upper lip.

"There. If you move quickly he won't notice."

"Pah! He is such a half-wit he wouldn't notice if I stood still in front of him."

Back down the hill raced Cuculann, with Jimmy close behind to cheer him on in the fight. The beast-man did not delay this time, but fell upon his assailant, roaring and bellowing. Cuculann danced lightly around him, pricking and cutting with swift, playful thrusts. At each cut the savage roared louder and brought his sword crashing to the ground. Cuculann laughed as he nimbly evaded the furious blows and his taunts and jeers enraged his opponent further. Finally maddened beyond sense, the beast-man threw himself upon Cuculann to crush the warrior with his monstrous weight. Legs astride and feet firm, Cuculann stood without moving, his sword held rigidly before him. The savage's angry cry died violently as he fell upon his enemy's weapon.

"Easy work," Cuculann said to Jimmy. "I am in great form today."

He wiped his sword clean on the grass, and sat down to wait for another challenger. Soon a man could be seen heading towards them, rather small and slight to Jimmy's surprise. But Cuculann didn't bother to stand up.

"Now remember our game, Jim. This is a satirist who comes before us. No weapons but words do they use. Their mockery can ruin the name of a warrior and bring everlasting shame upon his head. I must use cunning not force, for I can only defeat him if I trick him with words."

The satirist stopped a short distance from them. He had a mean, thin face and swaggered with his own importance.

"Put down your weapons," he cried in a shrill voice, "or lose your name."

"I would like to give them to you, but I cannot," Cuculann said politely.

"You are easily slandered, tight-fisted warrior," the satirist said with a cruel smile. His eyes glittered as he began to chant—

> "Shame to those who hold and keep,
> While children starve and women weep,
> Miser, collector, no gifts bestowed,
> Like handless worm and greedy toad—"

As the unfair words poured out like ooze, Jimmy grew hot and furious. Cuculann jumped up in a rage.

"Take my javelin, then, I give it to you!" he cried, and he flung the weapon, butt-end forward.

The satirist was thumped in the head and fell backwards, his legs kicking in the air.

"A knock-out of a gift you might say," Cuculann commented.

Red-faced and spluttering, the man picked himself off the ground and ran off without another word.

"I see what you did, Cucuc," Jimmy said, still laughing. "You had him from the beginning. By using the word 'give' you led him into that kind of slander, and then you gave him what he asked for. Right?"

"You'll play fidchell better after this."

Cuculann watched as the satirist disappeared from sight.

"They are a plague, these false poets. They make up for lack of skill by using the word to maim and dishonour. I wouldn't even waste my time killing him."

No more challengers arrived and the two returned to their campsite. Jimmy brought a gourd of ale from the chariot and they stretched out in front of the fire.

"How about that story you promised me?" he said to the warrior. "Why Ulster isn't with you in this fight?"

Cuculann took a long swallow of his beer and began the tale.

"In the days when the tribes of Ulster were young and the king's court was yet unnamed, Macha the goddess of the horse came into the land. She lived with the farmer Crunniuc mac Agnomain and she was above all other women in skill and knowledge. Crunniuc boasted of her constantly and though Macha warned him against such foolishness, he did not listen to her.

"On the feast of Bealtinne, at a fair in Ulster, they were racing horses and the King's rider won. Fool Crunniuc began to boast that his woman could run faster than any horse and the king heard of it and grew jealous. Though she was heavy with child, Macha was ordered to race against the King's horse. She begged and pleaded, and the women of Ulster cried with her, but no man would oppose the King. She was forced to run. She won, of course, but gave birth to two children at the finish. That is how the king's court received its name—Emain Macha, the twins of Macha. But the goddess screamed in her birth-pangs and placed a curse upon the land. From thence forth, whenever Ulster was in its greatest difficulties, it would be paralyzed like a woman giving birth and unable to help itself."

"So that's why the men of Ulster haven't joined you," Jimmy said. "But—that means they'll never come!"

The warrior shook his head.

"They will rise eventually as women do from child-bed, but it is a matter of time."

Jimmy thought about this for a while.

"How come you're not affected by the curse?"

"Three types of people are not; the women who pleaded for Macha, the children who took no part in the matter, and I, a son of the Sidhe, who cannot be bound by magic or curses."

"I couldn't imagine you being bound by anything," Jimmy said with a grin.

"Well I am," Cuculann laughed. "I am bound by a woman you might say, my wife Emer."

"You're married! At seventeen?"

"Have you no woman?"

"Not any serious ones. My sister says I'm a confirmed bachelor."

"You have a sister?"

"Rosemary. She's here in this world too, with Maeve's armies."

"Did she not mind you leaving to join me?" Cuculann asked.

Jimmy looked uneasy. "I didn't really get around to telling her. I was in a hurry to get back to you. I didn't think…"

Cuculann frowned. "That is your failing, James, I have noticed."

"We had a fight before I left," Jimmy said defensively. "I'm sure Fergus has told her where I am. There's no problem really. She's quite happy with Maeve's son and daughter."

Cuculann sat up suddenly and stared hard at Jimmy. A slow horror was dawning in his eyes.

"You should have told me this before. Do you not realize even now? The Connaught herald who came to us this morning will most surely have reported your presence with me. Your sister is in terrible danger."

Jimmy's face drained of blood as the full impact of Cuculann's words hit him. He was overcome with panic and his voice choked. "What have I done? I wasn't thinking. She…I… we've got to help her!" he cried.

Cuculann spoke sternly. "Do not lose your head, charioteer, and we shall save her's. We will have to go into the camp and find her, but we must not do it rashly."

They were still working on a plan when they spotted a man running towards them in the distance. As he neared the hill, Jimmy recognized Mac Roth, the messenger.

Cuculann's eyes narrowed with thought.

"Perhaps there will be something we can use here. Keep silent, James, when he arrives and I shall play my wiles."

The messenger climbed the hill and ran up to them.

"Mac Roth, you return again," Cuculann greeted him. "More bribes from Ailill, I hope?"

"He offers Finnabar, his daughter, if you will stay your hand till the men of Ulster come for the last battle. She will be your hostage to guarantee that the Connaught armies will not fight or plunder till that day. As a special mark of the King's esteem you may keep her as your woman when all is finished."

"Finnabar is already promised to many kings," Jimmy blurted out, despite Cuculann's orders.

Mac Roth stiffened. "It is the word of the King of Connaught."

"Very well, I accept," Cuculann said quickly. "Bring the girl to the ford after sunset and the King is to give her away."

When the messenger left, Cuculann told Jimmy to build the fire higher and prepare their meal. Then the warrior moved away to the edge of the hill where he sat alone and lost in thought.

Jimmy swallowed his frustration and did as he was told. His confusion and worry were all a jumble in his head. Everything was happening so fast and becoming too complicated and serious. But though he wasn't certain of what was going on, he trusted his friend and was prepared to obey him.

When the fire was burning well and Jimmy had laid out bread and meat for their supper, Cuculann rejoined him. The warrior's face looked clear and content and he smiled at Jimmy as he took up his food.

"The gods are with us. Events are moving in our favour and we must be wise to make use of them. They have no challenger to send tonight and will now resort to treachery. It is Ailill's intention, no doubt, to give Finnabar to me, but Maeve will corrupt it. There will be an ambush, I am certain, and with luck this means we will not have to go into the camp for your sister. We will be prepared for their attack and take as many hostages as possible to bargain for Rosemary's life."

As Jimmy listened to Cuculann, he felt sick with misery and guilt.

"What you're saying," he said quietly, "is that because of what I've done, you're going to walk right into a trap."

Cuculann put his hand on his friend's shoulder, and his voice was unusually gentle.

"James, your thoughtlessness you must suffer yourself. But I am happy to do this for your cause, when you have laboured so greatly for mine. This is the sign of our friendship, and we shall set out together with courage and hope."

Chapter Fifteen

he sound of horse's hooves woke Rosemary, and before she could figure out where she was or what she was doing, she heard Maine's voice calling her name.

"I'm here. I'm here!" she cried, running out of the stone-house.

Maine was leading his horse from the forest of Es Ruaid into the little clearing. As soon as he saw Rosemary, he ran towards her.

"You are well, despite my fears!"

He caught her up in his arms and held her tightly.

"Why did you leave me, love?" he murmured.

"I was trying to find the Druid," she said wearily. "I wanted to help my brother."

But her mind was confused with the broken images of a long dream. There was a shining man and a beautiful song, but she couldn't remember all of it. Everything was vague and uncertain, except Maine and the way he held her. Without protest, she was lifted onto his horse.

"Finnabar and I have been worried sick about you," he

scolded, as they rode through the forest. "She said you mentioned this place and I came as soon as I could."

Rosemary looked around her and wondered why she had been so afraid. In the clear light of morning, Es Ruaid looked simply old and overgrown.

"The Queen does not know you have been missing," Maine went on, "and we will not report it. The armies have crossed the Broad Ford and travelled through Cuailnge. We're now camped on the Plain of Conaille and I will get us there by a short route. Now what have you been doing for the past three days?"

"Three days?" she echoed.

She closed her eyes, unable to think clearly. Maine wrapped his cloak around her and held her close.

"I will sing you a little song," he said softly. "I thought of it when I came looking for you—

> First in a plain I hap did find her
> A stranger sweet and daring-oh
> Her long, dark hair fell all around her
> Her eyes as wild as the winds that blow.
>
> Wrapped in rose and silver shining,
> Shall I love this lady-oh?
> Or will she leave me sad and pining
> For a face as fair as the crystal snow?
>
> First I held her, then I kissed her
> A fire as bright as a starry-oh,
> In all my life I ne'er did meet
> Such a charming, playful lady-oh."

"That's lovely!" she cried.

He laughed at the surprise in her voice.

"Don't tell me I am the first man to write a song for you!"

"You wouldn't find the guys I know doing that," she said.

"It's strange men you're surrounded with Rose, that wouldn't sing to a beautiful woman. I'll think up another, then, though I'm not very good at it."

"Oh really?" she teased. "And were you always called 'honey-mouth', Milscothach?"

He was embarrassed and began to make excuses till she burst into laughter.

"Fie on you, Rose!" he cried, pretending to be hurt, "but if you must mock me to laugh, I will allow it. It is good to hear you laugh again."

They rode along happily, their low murmurs and laughter encouraged by the solitude of the countryside. But when they reached the camp at midday, they were surprised by the welcome that awaited them.

The Queen stood fully armed with her bodyguard close behind. Finnabar was beside her, with a face swollen and wearied from weeping. At a signal from Maeve, two men took hold of Rosemary and puller her roughly from Maine.

"What is the meaning of this?" Maine demanded.

His mother's face was white with fury and her eyes blazed.

"You have been taken in by a spy. You have been played for the fool, my son."

Rosemary looked at her in amazement.

"It was a fine show you put on, weeping and moaning for your brother," the Queen said with a tight smile.

"Jimmy's safe?" she cried eagerly.

"Yes, he is safe, false flower-face!" Maeve roared. "He

drives Cuculann's chariot and aids him in butchering my soldiers."

Overwhelmed by her joy and surprise, Rosemary didn't fully understand the Queen's words.

"He's been captured by the monster?" she asked anxiously.

"You madden me!" Maeve cried with fresh anger. "Caught and still weaving lies! Your brother is no captive of the warped one. My herald returned this morning from seeing Cuculann. There your brother sat, playing fidchell with him. He called himself Cuculann's servant, so do not try to worm your way out of this."

Rosemary was stunned. What was going on? Everything was happening too quickly and there was no time to think or understand. The Queen was saying worse things now.

"You, of course, have been helping them, meeting your traitorous brother and giving him information."

"That's not true! I haven't seen Jimmy since he disappeared."

"Liar! How else would they know our movements? But I will waste my breath on you no longer. You will die for this. You will die before the day is ended!"

Maine began to argue as Rosemary was dragged away, but the Queen turned on him.

"You have been bewitched by this lying sorceress. Do not compound your error, son, by defending her now and disobeying me."

At the furthest reaches of the camp, Rosemary was flung into a dark tent. Huddled on the cold ground, her cloak wrapped tightly around her, she peered into the darkness and wept. This was worse than the forest of Es Ruaid. At least then, she had hope. She cried out in fear of her death. Would no one stop it? But for some reason Jimmy had deserted her, and the Druid was nowhere to be found. She couldn't believe this was happening to her.

She heard a rustling at the door, and someone entered the tent.

"It is I," Finnabar said in a low voice. "I have brought you some food and a blanket."

Rosemary ate quickly, full of love for the girl.

"Oh Finn, my friend, my dear friend, I knew you would help me."

The girl gave her a frightened look and Rosemary stopped eating.

"You are going to help me get away, aren't you?"

"You know I can't," Finnabar said frantically. "Mother would know if I did. There is nothing I can do. I begged and pleaded with her. I tried not to tell her where you were, but she beat me. I couldn't help it. I can't help you now!"

"But you're my friend! I would do the same for you. I'm going to be killed. Can't you understand that? You mean you're going to let me die without lifting a hand to stop it?"

Rosemary was panic stricken. The gentility she had liked in Finnabar she now realized was weakness. Rosemary clutched at the girl's cloak as Finnabar stood up to leave.

"I must go, Rose. I've done all I can. I could be in trouble even for this. Please, you know I can't."

She was crying, but she kept shaking her head.

"Coward!" Rosemary screamed. "You wouldn't be hurt if you helped me. Your mother needs you. You're just too weak. And your brother too. You're all the same!"

Finnabar fled from the tent, leaving Rosemary convulsed in weeping, her hopes shattered once again. Finally there were no tears left; but in their wake came a quiet, relentless fury.

"They've all deserted me," she said to herself, as she thought of those who wouldn't stand by her in the worst moment of her life—her brother, Finnabar, Maine, the Druid. "I'll have to suffer it alone."

The anger and pride steadied her, rising up to defeat her fear, and as her determination grew, the words of the Harper came back to her, like an echo of his song. *There is hardship ahead, but you have the strength to face it.*

Hours later, when the soldiers came for Rosemary, they found her calm and ready. She was led into the camp now awash with the orange glow of sunset. Stiff and dishevelled from her imprisonment, she was brought before Maeve.

"She looks very dirty, does she not?" said the Queen to her daughter who stood miserable beside her. "Bring fresh clothes—your best—and have the attendants fill a tub of water."

Rosemary stared at Finnabar with cool contempt, but the girl hurried from the tent without looking at her.

"No, you did not succeed in casting your spell over my daughter," Maeve said. "She obeys me, not you. As for my son," she stopped and her eyes glittered with anger, "I have had to keep him bound and guarded all day. He dared raise his hand to me!"

Rosemary's worn face brightened. So he had tried to help her! He did love her. She straightened her aching back.

The Queen laughed, "You will not rule him long, sorceress. Your death will break the enchantment you hold over him and that will be soon enough."

"So you think," Rosemary said. Her voice was hoarse but steady. "He will always hate you for this. He loves me, not you, and he sees how evil you are."

Maeve flushed with rage and struck Rosemary across the face. The girl staggered back, but though she felt the shock of the blow, she drew herself up and smiled deliberately at the Queen.

"You are a ranting, raving coward. I've seen you hide from Cuculann beneath the shields of your men. You condemn others to death easily, but you run from your own."

"Get her out of my sight," Maeve screamed, "before I kill her with my own hands and ruin everything!"

Fighting back tears of pain and anger, Rosemary was pulled from the tent by the Queen's servants. Dully she endured the ministrations that followed as women bathed and dressed her. When they took her dagger from the soiled clothes, she came out of her stupor.

"Give that to me!" she said fiercely.

The attendants looked at her fearfully, then clasped the tiny weapon to her belt.

"White," she thought, looking down at the soft gown, the silver sandals on her feet. "They must intend to sacrifice me."

Images flashed through her mind. A stone table. A cold knife. Her own blood spattering over the white woollen robe. She shuddered and pushed the thoughts away. There would be time enough to face it. She was led back to the Queen's tent and found herself surrounded by warriors in wide, flowing cloaks.

"The hair must be covered," Maeve said, inspecting her. "Finnabar, your mantle with the hood, put it on her."

But Finnabar stood shaking and frightened. The Queen made a noise of disgust and pulled the mantle from her daughter to place it over Rosemary's shoulders. As she drew the hood over Rosemary's hair, she stopped and stared into the girl's impassive face.

"You are a sorceress and a spy," she said slowly, "but you have great courage. I give you this, my queenly brooch, as your death gift."

The huge brooch was curled and twisted like a serpent. Precious stones lay in the coils, winking with a cold, icy light. Maeve pinned it beneath Rosemary's chin and turned to Ailill.

"Your men are ready? Take her. This is the best of my plans yet. We have nothing to lose and everything to gain. See to it that the girl is killed whatever the outcome."

As the sun set and darkness descended over the hills, Jimmy and Cuculann set out for their meeting at the ford. Jimmy walked in silence, suffering a double guilt. That he had deserted his sister and put her in danger was bad enough, but now he was also endangering the life of his friend to save her.

"Perhaps there isn't deceit here," Cuculann said suddenly. "They have bound Finnabar to a standing stone to show their good faith, and she wears Maeve's brooch. Who else would have the Queen's ornament?"

"Your keen eyes again," Jimmy said, as he squinted towards the ford.

He could barely make out the dim shapes in the wavering light of their torches.

"Is the King there?" he asked Cuculann.

"No," the warrior said, his mouth tightening with anger. "That is a younger body dressed in Ailill's colours, and those beside him who should be attendants are fighting men."

Jimmy swore and put his hand on his scabbard. "Should we try to capture Finnabar?"

Cuculann wasn't listening. His rage was already bursting inside him and he leapt forward with a great cry.

"You will all die for breaking the pact of single combat!"

Cuculann ran with ferocious speed towards the ford, as the group of men drew the weapons they had concealed in their cloaks. With a clash of metal and shouts, the battle began.

Jimmy had drawn his sword and was running to join the fight, when something caught his eye. He stopped in cold and sudden fear. The figure tied to the stone had begun to struggle as the men fought around her. Jimmy strained to see in the dimness of the fallen torches. Her hood fell back and the long black hair streamed over her face.

"Rosemary," he whispered.

He was faint with shock. He couldn't believe it.

Cuculann's rampage was almost over. The imposters lay dead upon the ground and now the warrior advanced towards the girl, his sword raised above his head.

"No, Cucuc!" Jimmy screamed. "She's my sister!"

He knew it was no use. When Cuculann was in a blood-lust he didn't stop till he had killed everything before him. In agony, Jimmy watched as the distance between Rosemary and Cuculann narrowed. What could he do? His heart pounded and his blood rang in his ears. Deep inside he knew what he had to do and it pressed against him till he could hardly breathe and his knees shook. He would have to run between them. He would have to let Cuculann kill him and, dying before him, beg for Rosemary's life. He closed his eyes and broke into a cold sweat. He had not expected it to come like this. So sudden. And by Cuculann's hand. It would be painful. It would be horrible. He was not ready for it.

"I can't. I can't," he whispered.

Every second he stood there would make the decision harder, would make it impossible. If he stood there a little longer, it would be over and he could do nothing. In his mind he saw Rosemary covered in blood, Rosemary screaming as the sword slashed through her.

"I must. I have to. Oh, help me. Help me," he prayed.

Chapter Sixteen

y the edge of the ford, in the shadow of a giant oak tree, two Druids stood watching the spectacle.

"It is as the vision foretold," one spoke.

The other did not reply but his eyes grew darker as he watched.

"You will have to save the girl," the speaker urged, "or you will be bound here with no hope of return."

"I am well aware of that," Peter said calmly, "but as I came in three and must go in three, I cannot act without the three."

"The boy is not involved."

"He is there."

A cry suddenly reached them, pained and desperate but ringing with triumph. A slight figure ran across the ford towards the girl and the warrior.

"Now I can act," Peter said, and he stepped out from the shadow of the oak tree and began to sing in a strange and beautiful tongue.

Rosemary strained against her bonds as the terrible man

bore down upon her. Jimmy ran towards Cuculann, heart bursting but ready for death. For an age-long moment they froze in their places, three people caught in a circle of love and fear. Then a mist-breath of pale colours and flashes of light enfolded them. Rosemary and Jimmy felt themselves being lifted from the ground and carried upwards till there was nothing but blue sky all around them. They hung in the air, shocked and senseless, till a Voice boomed in their minds.

"This is not a dream. This is not your death. Fly. Fly to the forest! Cuculann can reach you even in this form."

They did not stop to think of what or where they were. The Voice commanded them to flee. With a rush of wings and wind, they spread themselves upon the air and searched for the green tree-tops that would shelter them; for they knew instinctively that their Enemy was below, the Human who kills the creatures of the sky. Spears whistled by them as they strained to reach the place of safety.

"No good. No good," the Voice cried. "Cuculann still follows. To the ground!"

They fell with a sickening thud to the hard earth. Once again their bodies were changing. Four-legged, brutish, they crashed through the underbrush with a speed that dazed them. They were urged on by the cries of the Voice and their own natural fear, for they knew that the Stalker, the Boar-Hunter, was close behind. Their hearts beat wildly as a deadly rain of javelins fell around them. They plowed through the forest, running and running with nowhere to hide.

"To the river, to the river," the Voice commanded.

With a slithering splash they slid over the bank and down

into the silvery depths. They flickered in the sunlit water, slicing through the element as they darted downstream. A dark shadow blocked their path and massive beats on the water told them that the Eater of Fish was above them.

"No good at all," the Voice said wearily. "Cuculann cannot be fooled by magic. We must go where his fury cannot follow. Back. Back to our own place."

One moment there was sunny water and a dark fear, the next a whirlpool opened before them and great tossing waves sucked them inward. The mad rushing spun and pushed them, beat and changed them: talons curled, gills quivered, snouts crushed, tails twisted.

"What am I? Who am I?" they cried in the painful whirling.

With a crash they fell bruised and battered to the ground.

"I am me. I am Rosemary," the girl said.

"I am me. I am Jimmy," the boy said.

They lay without moving, slowly gathering their splintered selves into one whole piece.

"A bit rough, I'm afraid. The haste made it so," the Voice said.

It was no longer in their minds, but outside where voices belonged, and now it was familiar.

"Peadar," Rosemary said, as she pulled herself from the ground.

Jimmy stood up holding his head. They were in the field of their uncle's farm. The lake and the spinney glowed palely around them.

"We're home! We're home!" they cried, hugging each other in joy.

"Of course you're home," said Peter crossly. "I am not a beginner."

He stood over them in his Druidical garb. "And I don't want to hear any complaints. You brought it all upon yourselves by sneaking up on me last night."

With that he strode off, leaving them to gape after him speechless.

"You're still alive!" Jimmy said. "And so am I!"

He felt his arms and legs to be certain. They hugged again, overjoyed to see each other safe and sound.

"So here ye's be!" their uncle's stern voice came behind them. "And dressed in costume no less. What kind of shenanigans are these? Your aunt has been worried sick about ye's. Playing games and us thinkin' ye's had run away! Your da said ye's were apt to be wild, but have ye no thought for others at all?"

They hung their heads in shame, but said nothing. They couldn't begin to explain without making matters worse.

"Oh I'm so glad to see you Uncle Patsy!" Rosemary suddenly cried, and she hugged him tightly.

His eyes softened though they were still puzzled.

Jimmy looked directly at his uncle and spoke honestly.

"This looks bad Patsy, and we're sorry for upsetting you and Aunt Ella. We can't tell you what we've been doing, and that makes it look even worse. I can only ask you to trust us. We haven't been doing anything wrong."

Patsy gave him a long, hard look then nodded slowly.

"I trust ye's. You're my sister's children and I know ye's wouldn't be lyin' to me. We'll say no more on the matter. There's work to be done and we should be gettin' to it."

They fell over their words trying to thank him and promising to behave. He shooed them out of the field laughing and shaking his head.

"Foreign childer'," he thought to himself. "What do they be up to at'all?"

They hurried back to the house, thankful that Ella was not in the kitchen. In a confused rush they changed into jeans and sweaters and hid their weapons and clothes in the wardrobe of Rosemary's room. When their aunt came in from feeding the chickens, she found them sitting down to their breakfast. They began again to make apologies and excuses, trying hard not to lie in the process.

"We were at the lake," Rosemary said. "We lost track of time."

"Jet-lag," Jimmy piped in. "You don't know if it's day or night for a while."

"Ye poor things," Ella said kindly, and they felt awful. "But if that's all it was, sure you'll be gettin' over it soon. Patsy and I were only afraid... well, no mind. Everything's grand now."

When she left them alone they looked at each other thoughtfully.

"I take it we've only been missing for a few hours, then," Jimmy said finally.

"Nothing surprises me anymore," Rosemary said with a sigh. "It was all Peadar's magic and every one of those days happened in one night, last night, when we followed him out to the lake."

She ate slowly, still confused by the speed of events and the fact that she was back in the world she thought she would never see again.

"I think, Jim, we better be extra good and work really hard so Patsy will forget about this. He was so kind about finding us in the field with those clothes on and all. He could have had a fit and demanded explanations, or worse, phoned Dad and told him we were acting weird."

"Cripes. I never thought of that. Dad would murder us."

Rosemary winced, "Don't use that word. Well then, let's wash up and get to work."

"That's okay, I'll do it. By the way, Ro, will you teach me to cook when you've got the time?"

"What?"

"I mean it. Don't ask questions. Just will you?"

She left the house laughing. Everything was rather funny and wonderful. She looked at the farmyard loving every bit of it — the old barn, the chickens scratching in the grass, the flowers growing along the walls of the house. It wasn't a place she knew well, but for the moment it was home.

"Where everything is safe and normal and real," she sang.

Chapter Seventeen

immy swore as his scythe caught a clump of soil and threw it into the air. He looked around quickly to see if his uncle had seen, but Patsy was busy giving instructions to Rosemary. They were in the field above Drumoor, cutting the long grass so it would dry in the sun and make hay for Patsy's winter feed. They had spent most of the week learning how to handle the long scythes and Jimmy was convinced it was a hopeless cause. Again and again their uncle had moved across the meadow, slicing the tall, damp grass till it lay like shorn hair in a scattered row behind him. Again and again, they had tried to copy him, holding awkwardly the curved wooden handle to swing the blade in a half-arc through the grass. But they were cutting wildly and missing half of it, tossing up earth and nearly severing their own legs.

"Sure ye's can't expect to be doin' it right for a while yet," Patsy said encouragingly. "But aren't ye's a pair of strong ones for city children?"

"Good thing we went on the Tain," Jimmy said to his sister when Patsy moved away, "or this would kill us."

"Hmm," was all she said, and he dropped the subject.

She hadn't mentioned the adventure since their return and Jimmy suspected she had blocked it out of her mind completely.

At noon they went back to the farmhouse for lunch and found Ella dressed in her best clothes.

"We'll be goin' into town today, Rose," she said, "to get ye a frock for mass."

As her aunt turned to lift the dinner from the stove, Rosemary rolled her eyes and whispered to Jimmy.

"Sounds like fun. A dress. And for church. Ugh!"

"Anything to get out of work," her brother said.

Ballinamore was a little town nestled snugly in the heart-hills of County Leitrim. Its tiny doll-like houses were gaily painted in whites, pinks and blues, and lace curtains and bright flowers fluttered in every window. Pubs and shops lined the main street, the proprietors' names across the doorways calling out the oldest families of the district — Prior's Bar and Grocery, McGovern's Bootshop, McKiernan's Victuallers, Dolan's Public House, Delahoyde's Hotel. Rosemary couldn't help catching her aunt's good spirits as they strolled through the winding streets, looking in the shop windows and stopping to chat with Ella's friends.

"And is this the little girrul from America?" they would say.

"Canada," Rosemary would answer.

She had given up hope of finding a dress that she liked, when she spotted one in a shop window, and they went in to try it on. The dress hung in soft, loose folds to her knees and the long narrow sleeves clung to her arms. It was a little old-fashioned but the rose-coloured wool appealed to her.

"It looks well on ye," Ella said admiringly, "and it goes with your dark hair."

Rosemary sighed, "It reminds me of a dress I wore once, for someone special," and before she could stop them the words echoed through her mind, *Wrapped in rose and silver shining.*

She pushed the memory away. She didn't want to remember any part of that other world or the people in it. But when she returned home she took out the clothes and weapons they had brought back from the Tain and spread them upon her bed.

"Treasures," she murmured softly. "Beautiful and alien treasures."

She lingered over the strange, shining articles—the white gown and long mantle she had worn to the ford, the Queen's exquisite brooch, Jimmy's hard, gleaming sword, her own finely-worked dagger. With sudden inspiration she opened her paintbox and began a series of sketches. There was Maine upon his horse singing to her, and Finnabar with an armful of flowers laughing merrily. She drew Jimmy looking every bit the warrior beside Fergus in their great chariot. Then Maeve, holding her sword like a goddess of war and battle.

"She was magnificent," Rosemary thought, looking at the picture of the Queen. "Even I have to admit that. A giantess in full and furious glory."

She looked fondly at the portrait of Finnabar. She had

painted the girl in watercolours, light hues of green and gold.

"Poor Finn. You were too soft. You weren't cut out for the Tain. It wasn't your fault you couldn't handle it."

By the time Rosemary was finished her work, she could hear everyone in the kitchen preparing for supper.

"Come down Rosie," her aunt called. "Your brother has made a stew and, heaven help us, he says we have to eat it."

She came down the stairs to find Ella and Patsy in fits of laughter and Jimmy standing red-faced over a huge pot on the stove.

"I'm only as good as my teacher," he was saying. "Ro says no one can ruin a stew."

"We'll soon find out about that, brother of mine," and she made a face as he handed her a heaping plateful.

"It looks all right," Patsy said doubtfully.

They tasted the food carefully as Jimmy waited for the verdict.

"I think it's grand," Ella declared, giving her favourite judgement on good things.

The rest agreed, and they ate till the pot was empty.

Jimmy looked very pleased with himself and began to brag.

"Shows how useful I am compared to you, sis. What were you doing in your room all afternoon?"

"I was working. A few sketches. Would anyone like to see them?"

They pushed back their chairs and Ella filled their cups with tea and brought out the tin of biscuits. Patsy lit his pipe as Rosemary brought the pictures from her room.

"They're rough sketches, plans for oil paintings," she explained as she handed them around.

Jimmy looked at them eagerly, exclaiming over each but saying nothing as he caught her glance.

"What an imagination you have, girl," her uncle said, admiring them. "But you pinched this one, now, from the new pound note."

"What do you mean?" she asked laughing.

"It's Queen Maeve isn't it?"

Jimmy's cup fell into his saucer with a clatter.

"You know her?" Rosemary whispered.

"I know *of* her. The great Queen of Connaught who wanted the Brown Bull of Ulster."

A silence settled over the table.

"Then you know of Cuculann?" Jimmy asked, his eyes wide.

Ella started to laugh and Patsy looked at him quizzically.

"First cooking and now Irish history. You've unusual interests, me boyo."

"History!" they cried together.

"I wasn't much in school meself," Patsy went on, "but I know the names of the ancient kings and queens and of course I know about Cuculann, the great hero of Ireland. There's a statue of him in the Post Office up in Dublin, ye know."

"If it's history," Rosemary said in amazement, "when?"

"Now that I can't be tellin' ye. Before Christ, I'm thinkin'."

"It's not really known," Ella added. "Some say they were the fairy people and not of this world at'all. We only know about them through the old stories and legends."

"Let's see the pound note," Jimmy said eagerly.

Patsy reached into his pockets and drew out some rumpled bills. Smoothing one out, he handed it to the boy.

Jimmy whistled. It wasn't an exact replica of the Queen, but it was what he would call an 'idea' of her; a massive head of long, thick hair, a high and majestic countenance.

"She looks pretty tame in this picture," he commented, "considering she's usually screaming with rage."

"Now how would you be knowin' that?" Patsy asked with a great laugh.

Rosemary gave her brother a dig.

"He's just talking about nothing," she said hurriedly. "He has a habit of doing that."

After they washed the dishes, Rosemary and Jimmy sauntered out to the barn where they often sat to watch the twilight.

"So what do you think of that," Rosemary said. "Time-travel. Ireland's past."

"Not necessarily," her brother said slowly. "Aunt Ella said they could belong to another race," and he echoed his friend's words — "There are other worlds alongside Ireland in the same time but not the same place, and sometimes they touch."

"Why Jimmy, I do believe you're getting thoughtful in your old age."

"Cuculann told me that."

She shuddered. "That horrible man."

"He wasn't, I mean, *isn't*, Ro. You don't know him the way I do. He's full of laughs and jokes, and he taught me a lot of things. He's so alone against all his enemies."

"That's all right for you to say. He wasn't trying to kill *you*."

"He would have killed me that time, you know, I'm sure of it. But it wouldn't have been his fault. He goes that way when he's fighting. He has to. It's the way he survives."

"Well, the only memory I have of him is an awful one and I can't get rid of it."

"I noticed you didn't do a picture of him."

"No and I won't."

They sat looking out at the hills in silence. Jimmy bit his lip.

"If I don't mention Cucuc," he said wistfully, "will you talk with me about the other parts?"

She was about to refuse point blank when she looked at his face and relented.

"Oh all right. Do you want me to bring out the stuff we brought back?"

"Great idea, and your drawings too. I'll get a flashlight."

Rosemary wrapped the clothes and weapons into a tight bundle and place her sketches on top. She hurried through the kitchen with her arms full, smiling at Patsy and Ella as she went.

"Just chatting in the barn," she said as she went out the door.

No more had been said about the day Patsy found them in the field and she thought it best to leave it that way. Back in the barn, they spread everything around them and talked and talked about the adventure. "Remember this?" and "What about the time…". They went on for hours.

When Rosemary described what had happened to her after Jimmy left the camp, her brother's face grew serious.

"I should never have left you like that. I just thought you'd be...no, I don't have an excuse. It was a really rotten thing to do."

"Well, it's over, so we'll forget about it. You tried to save me that time and I appreciate it."

"I wonder what all that stuff about the Harper meant?"

"I've tried to figure it out," she shrugged, "but I can't. Can't draw it either. Everything was full of light. More magic, I guess."

"Yeah, it was all magic, Peter's magic, and somehow we got into it though he hates our guts."

They both laughed.

"I know what you mean," Rosemary said. "He's positively antisocial. But I'd love to do a picture of him in that get-up. A Druid," she said dreamily. "A dark wizard."

"Has he talked to you since we got back?" Jimmy asked her.

"Not a word. Might as well not be here for all that I've seen of him. Patsy said he was fixing the fences this week, on the far side of the lake. I've spotted him wandering around like a shadow now and then, but that's it."

"I tried to talk to him today, when you were in town."

"Jimmy, you didn't! Where did you get the nerve?"

"I was worried about, well never mind, I said I wouldn't mention his name. Anyway, I asked him about you-know-who and if he was all right. Peter just turned his back on me. I stood there like an idiot till he finally said something."

"What did he say?" she asked breathlessly.

"He said we couldn't go back unless there were three of us."

Rosemary's face froze and she looked away. She began to gather up the articles and her etchings.

"Ro...," Jimmy chose his words carefully. "If we had the chance, just the mere chance, of going back... would you?"

She looked him straight in the eye.

"Certainly not!"

That night Jimmy lay beneath his blankets in the barn and looked out at the stars that winked on the end of his toes.

"Ella must be right and Patsy wrong. It can't be history. It must be another world, a world that's still going on right now. If it's history—it can't be—but if it is, then...then he's long dead and buried. My greatest friend!"

Chapter Eighteen

hen Sunday arrived, Rosemary and Jimmy found they had no chores to do as no one in the Donovan household worked on that day. Jimmy had to put on a tie and jacket and Rosemary wore her new dress. It was an easy lazy day, a day for writing letters home and going for walks, or just relaxing and waiting for Ella's roast beef dinner. After dinner they were told they were going into town for one o'clock mass.

"It's a folk mass or so they call it," their aunt explained. "For the young people."

Jimmy tugged at his collar, trying to catch a breath over the knotted tie. Without thinking, Patsy did the same. Their faces shone pink over the stiff white shirts and freshly brushed suits. Rosemary stood around awkwardly, being very conscious of her bare knees. Only Ella was comfortable, looking smart and prim in a hat of yellow flowers. She inspected the three of them carefully and declared each fit for mass.

"Right, let's be off," said Patsy, ushering them out to the

car. "Ladies in the back where you won't be creasin' your frocks."

"We'd better hurry, Pat," Ella said. "We'll be needin' a place to park and, Lord bless us, there's the rain."

"Don't be worryin', love, I'll get ye to the church on time." Patsy winked at his nephew. "It'd be this every Sunday now. The little woman is very religious-minded."

"I'm knowin' what's right and what's wrong," Ella argued mildly, "and it's not right to be walkin' into mass when it's half over."

"How long does it go on for?" Jimmy wanted to know.

"No more than an hour."

The teenagers groaned inwardly. Their parents didn't practise a religion and they had never been to church. As far as they were concerned the whole idea was horribly boring.

The sky had clouded over and rain drizzled down as they drove into Ballinamore. The church bells pealed the quarter-hour and they ran through the wet streets and up the steps to the chapel. Inside they were enveloped in the rustling of raincoats and the hot, damp breath of the gathering. Everything was warm, brown and hushed. Ella nudged them into a front pew.

Rosemary's eyes were wide as she stared around her in awe. Marble pillars rose to the dark recesses of the roof like a forest of great, shining trees. The prismed windows glittered with bright, coloured images of beautiful people and strange, mythical beasts. There was a high altar covered in white lace and a golden cup that gleamed in the dim candlelight.

Rosemary turned to her brother. "There's magic here. Can you feel it?"

He shrugged and whispered back, "It's nice, not what I expected, but what do you mean?"

She wasn't sure herself. It was a feeling welling up inside her, and it stayed with her throughout the mass.

When they came out of the church, the rain had stopped and the sun was shining in the puddles. The music and singing and strange words still rang in Rosemary's head. She felt odd in a funny, pleasant sort of way. When they reached the farm she changed into her jeans and went for a walk through the fields. The raindrops sparkled in the meadowgrass like liquid crystal. Warm breezes played around her, and she wandered through the spinney and down to Lake Drumoor.

"Magic, magic everywhere," she said to herself.

The feeling was so strong it was like a veil she could touch. It seemed as if pale shadows danced in the sunlight around her, whispering and beckoning; the grey-eyed Druid, the proud warrior-queen, romantic Maine, gentle Finnabar—all the people of that other world—so different, so alive, so bright. Whether good or bad, they filled her with excitement. They made *her* feel fierce, high, and full of the courage of life.

"It was like walking among gods," she said sadly, "and I'm too afraid to go back to them."

Where would she ever find people like that again?

"You are confused and in pain."

The voice startled her and she turned to find Peter standing beside her.

"I want to go back, but I'm frightened."

"You no longer hate Finnabar?"

"No. I understand now what fear and weakness can do to a person and I think she suffered for it."

"She did," he sighed, "and in ways you will never know of."

He sat down on the dock and she looked at him curiously. The familiar lines of anger and hostility were gone from his face, but he seemed weary and forlorn. She was no longer in awe of him, but there was still something there, something about him that made him different, aloof and untouchable.

"How old are you?" she was surprised to hear herself ask.

He spoke slowly and in such a low voice, that she sat down beside him in order to hear.

"Though I was born to this world twenty-one years ago, I am older, far older. My head is full of secrets. From one life to another, one shape to another, I have been many and perhaps all things. I am scattered on the winds, over time, and through the worlds. Though I know parts, others press against me, and I am at a loss to understand or know them."

"That must be terrible," she said, finding sympathy for him.

"It is the lack of knowledge that pains me, not the seeking itself. I will be whole one day when I have gathered the parts together."

"Can you help me make my decision?" she asked him.

"Not long ago I would have said that your problems were your own to handle," he said quietly, "but you and your brother have taught me a lesson.

"I have been a Druid lost without clan and companions. For years I have searched in the dark places, by water and high ground, in the caves, and beneath the stars. I journeyed to the sacred grove of Derrydruel, the holy well of Tobernadree and the high hill of Knocknadrooa. So many times I came to the door and it refused to open, though I could hear the voices of my brothers calling to me on the other side. Then I came to this lake."

Peter looked over the waters of Drumoor which gleamed and rippled in the sunny mist.

"In ages past," he murmured, "Drumoor was called by another name, though it is remembered in this new one. Loughnadrooa. The Lake of the Druids. Beneath its smooth sands lie the bones of my brethren."

Rosemary shivered and he smiled wryly.

"Druids do not die, Rose, only their bodies. Their souls migrate to new forms.

"I came to this place because I felt it was here that entrance would be granted to me. But though the door shone with fire, it did not open and once again I was lost, cast out from what I sought."

"You got through finally," Rosemary pointed out.

"Yes, and only because you and your brother were here. At first I was angry, but it seems I have much to learn. It was a sign and a warning to me. I have spent too much time inside myself. I can neither seek nor find without others to guide me. I realize that now though my pride fought against it."

"Yes," Rosemary said, slowly remembering, "*Seek for self and ye be blind.*"

Peter looked at her and the sadness in his eyes, in his features, set free her memory like a flood of light.

"He looked just like you! The Harper! Only different. I mean…I thought it was you at first!"

Peter's eyes widened with surprise.

"You met him? The Harper of Cain Bile?"

"I did and…" she grew excited, "but it was like a dream. Whenever I try to catch it, it disappears. He said so many things that I didn't understand. Part of you—yes—he said he was part of you and you were looking for him, but you weren't looking properly." Rosemary stopped to catch her breath. Peter had closed his eyes and his face was pale. She had upset him, she realized. "I'm sorry, Peadar, I…"

"Do not apologize," he said. "You are right. My heart was closed and bitter, and that is why I did not find him. However, I saw him in a vision, though he was far away, the vision that revealed your peril."

"He told me that," Rosemary said. "He sent the vision, and when you decided to help us, you were able to see him." She was fascinated. It was all so strange and mysterious, the life of this man. "So he's one of the parts of you that's scattered everywhere?"

Peter nodded, "And still he eludes me."

Rosemary thought for a while and then made her decision.

"Well," she said determinedly, "we'll just have to go back and find him again."

He looked at her strangely, and if she hadn't been full of her new idea she would have recognized the remorse in his eyes.

"You have forgiven your brother and Finnabar for deserting you. Have you found it in your heart to forgive me?"

She was surprised.

"I never blamed you for what happened! We were the ones who followed you that night."

He shook his head with a pained smile. "I begin to realize, Rose, why it was you that came to take my hand. Your innocence makes my guilt all the greater."

His humility made her uncomfortable and she wasn't sure if she understood what he was saying.

"Why did you take us into that world anyway?" she asked, changing the subject.

"I did not take you. Each of us took the other, in a sacred triad."

"I don't understand. It was all your magic wasn't it?"

"You have power of your own." He looked at her in a peculiar way. "Everyone does."

He sighed and stood up. "I am only confusing you with my words. Such knowledge is best learned from within. As for your fear of that other world—it is rooted in my neglect. I did not look after you when we were there last, but if you do consent to return, I promise to stay by you. No harm will come to you unless you agree to it yourself."

Rosemary jumped up. "I'll tell Jimmy. He'll be so happy. We'll all go back together this time!"

"You will have to wait a while," he cautioned her. "It is not an easy thing travelling through the worlds. I will call you when I am ready."

Chapter Nineteen

he days passed with no word or sign from Peter and they began to wonder anxiously if he had changed his mind. Then on Saturday, when they were sitting down to lunch, Patsy came into the kitchen laughing and shaking his head.

"There's some days I wonder whether I'm comin' or goin'," he said. "I was workin' away with the lad—those fences'll be up in no time—a quiet bit of workin' and he always quiet, when doesn't he turn around to me and say, 'it's a fine day.' Just like that. I nearly dropped me hammer. Then before I could put my eyes back in my head, he asks if he can take the two Americans fishin'."

Rosemary and Jimmy almost cried out with excitement and nodded to each other knowingly.

"Oh we've become great friends with Peadar," Rosemary said with a happy smile.

"'Peadar' is it now? And you be callin' him by his name in Irish?" Patsy's eyes twinkled. "Ye's wouldn't be courtin'?"

"Good heavens, no!"

She was shocked at the very suggestion. Peter was like—well, you just didn't think of him that way.

"I'm glad ye's are makin' friends with him," Ella said. "I was always thinkin' he needed some young people to be with."

"I said I'd ask ye's," Patsy went on, "so if ye's are of a mind for it, wash up the delph and be off. He said he'd meet ye's at the lake."

They were crossing the fields to Lake Drumoor when Rosemary noticed that Jimmy carried something else besides his fishing gear.

"Okay, what's under the blanket," she demanded.

Her brother looked sheepish as she flipped the corner of the cloth. There was a glint of grey metal.

"My first sword," he hurried to explain. "I have to take it with me. After all, Fergus..."

She stopped his excuses with a giggle and pulled her dagger from her back pocket.

"To clean the fishes," she said with a wink.

They were still laughing when they joined Peter by Lake Drumoor. He did not smile, but his nod was friendly as he greeted them.

"We will move to the far side of the lake. Your uncle is a patient man, but we must not push his kindness too far. It is best not to involve others in such doings."

They tramped over the hills to the furthest and most secluded corner of Lake Drumoor. The sun was shining all around them and a pair of swans sailed on the surface of the water. It was a lovely day for fishing but that was the last thing on their minds. With growing excitement, they hid their uncle's fishing gear in the bushes and waited for the Druid's instructions.

"You will have to float on the water," he said, "with your face to the sky."

Rosemary and Jimmy looked uneasily at the lake. Only a foot from shore the bottom disappeared into dark and unknown depths.

"You must trust me," Peter said quietly.

"We do," they said, and without further hesitation, they waded in.

As they lay back on the cool water, they heard Peter's voice ring out.

"I call on the sun and the moon, the dew and all the colours of the earth. I call on all elements visible and invisible, and every element on heaven and earth. We seek passage. We three seek entrance to the worlds within worlds."

As his words reached them, Rosemary and Jimmy were slowly submerged in a watery darkness.

Jimmy opened his eyes and found himself blinded by colour and light. He was rushing through a vista of vivid chaos. Colours, shapes and sounds melted and ran together. One second he was up looking down, the next he was down looking up. One moment he was crowded and squeezed by a hundred unknown forms, and the next he was flying alone through a vast emptiness. Then out of the mists a lovely girl stepped towards him. Around her shoulders fell a mane of dark hair, black as the night and sparkling with clusters of stars. Her eyes were blue and silver like a cloudy sky. Her slender white arms opened to embrace him. All the women he had ever loved shone in her face like a many-coloured mirror: his mother, his sister, the soft, pretty girls he had glimpsed and dreamed of. He reached out to touch her.

"Not here," the Druid's voice came into his mind. "This is not the place you are going to."

A tinkle of laughter chimed through his head.

"Perhaps another time, James," she said, and her voice was like the rustle of leaves on a summer day.

Jimmy sighed as she faded back into the mists.

"She was something else," he said to no one in particular.

Rosemary's journey was different from her brother's. For a moment she panicked as the water engulfed her, but she could hear Peter singing and she quieted her fears.

"I'm sinking fast," she thought, but no, it was upward she was travelling.

Rosemary opened her eyes and saw that she was submerged, not in water, but in a great black void that was neither cold nor tangible.

"Space?" she thought in surprise.

She could see star-streams and suns, shining moons and pale planets, all rippling and bobbing in the dimness. Like a bead on a silver wire, she was racing through infinity. Jimmy and Peter were nowhere to be seen. She was alone in the great shadow of the universe.

At first Rosemary felt compelled to drive herself onward. But after a while the stillness and beauty of the Deep called out to her and she lost all desire to leave it. Ages seem to pass and she lay without moving or thinking, listening in her heart to the strange, blissful silence of eternity. Then something began to prod at her. She tried to ignore it but the jabs grew insistent and finally painful. There was no one near her but she knew, somehow, that it was the Druid, and with a sigh of regret she began to move once more. In a great surge and burst of dark spray, she rose above the black ocean and floated on her back. A brilliant light flooded over her, warm and golden, tender and loving.

"God?" she thought happily.

"If you don't get out of there," her brother yelled, "you'll catch cold!"

Spluttering and flailing, Rosemary climbed out of the water and onto the shore.

"That was better than the last voyage," Peter commented.

"We're back," Rosemary whispered, as she looked around the ford. "There's the stone they tied me to." She turned her face away.

"There is no one here," Peter told her, "but this is where we left and, therefore, where we begin again." He stiffened suddenly, "Cuculann is in terrible anguish. We must go to him quickly."

"How?" Jimmy cried.

"What little faith you have in me," he said drily.

The Druid had no sooner spoken than Jimmy felt himself shrinking and shrivelling till his arms touched the ground and he rested on all fours. He lifted his head to the air, suddenly aware of the intensity of sound and smell. He sprang forward, his hind legs incredibly strong and agile. He felt small and helpless, yet he knew he had great power and speed in that smallness.

Something tickled his nose, an odour that spoke in his mind the name "Cuculann".

"You can sense your friend," the Druid said. "Go to him. We will follow."

Jimmy bound forward with no need of urging. He traced the odour as easily as if it were a light on the road ahead of him. The wind rushed through him as he ran. The ground bobbed and heaved beneath him. He could hear the insects humming and small creatures calling out to him as they scurried through the grass, but though he understood what they were saying, he didn't stop in his flight towards Cucu-lann. He followed the scent for miles till he came to a lone hilltop dark against the cheerless grey sky. With a great churning and twisting, he unravelled to his own shape and height.

There before him lay the scattered ashes of a dead fire and lying beside it, the broken body of Cuculann. Jimmy let out a cry. A tremor ran through the dying warrior and he opened his eyes, dazed with pain and tears.

"Jim," Cuculann whispered through clenched teeth, "you have come back to me."

Chapter Twenty

immy stared in shock at the state of his friend. Cuculann's limbs were twisted and broken. His body bled darkly through great, gaping wounds. It looked as if he had been lying there for some time, alone and in terrible agony.

Jimmy heard a noise behind him and watched in a daze as two small hares changed to the forms of his sister and the Druid.

"We're too late!" he cried to them. "Look at him. He's dying!"

The Druid knelt quickly beside Cuculann and examined his wounds.

"There is nothing I can do," he said wearily. "He has passed the point of healing."

Jimmy's voice shook with grief and bewilderment, "There must be something we can do. We can't just let him die."

Rosemary looked down at the warrior with pity. Her last

encounter was forgotten, washed away in the blood and suffering she saw before her.

"You have so many powers," she pleaded with Peter. "You must be able to help him. Please. Let us help too, in any way we can."

She saw him hesitate.

"It is not in me to heal with power," he said, but his uncertainty was more obvious now. She could see that he was trembling.

"What about the three of us," she insisted. "You said we have power together."

Peter nodded reluctantly, "We are a triad. That is the sacred number, the key to all mysteries."

"Then we *can* do something together!" Jimmy cried, realizing what was being said.

Rosemary was watching the Druid closely. There was something wrong. His agitation was growing and she suddenly knew why.

"You're afraid?" she whispered.

He stared back at her.

"You are asking for the power of life over death. The greatest power. The most awesome."

"He's not dead yet," Jimmy argued.

"He has already begun to journey outward," Peter answered. "He is already leaving his body."

Rosemary moved closer to the Druid and reached out to touch his arm.

"But he hasn't left yet? Even in our own world, people have been brought back though they nearly died. We must try."

"You don't understand. You will have to bear the hardship of it."

"Anything. We'll do anything," Jimmy said urgently.

"So be it," the Druid said finally, and the intensity of his face, of his eyes, was sharp and glittering. Shadows and fitful flashes of light were flickering over him. His eyes were changing, the pale grey diffusing and melting into white. "You demand this of me, and I shall grant it. Then I demand of you the strength to hold the triad together."

"We'll give it," they swore.

The Druid held out his hands so that the three were clasped in a circle away from Cuculann. The air around them began to dim, thickening with darkness and liquid shadow. Rosemary shivered as she sensed the power that the Druid was gathering to them. Then they felt it, slivers of pain, like lightning, shooting through them.

Rosemary cried out, and then Jimmy. Their first thought was to escape, to run away before it got worse.

"Don't break the circle!" the Druid cried. "The pain is Cuculann's. We must hold it for him, till he finds the strength to live."

Rosemary and Jimmy clung harder, to each other and the Druid, swaying back and forth as the torment increased.

"It's for Cuculann," Jimmy told himself triumphantly, as he met each onslaught, each new wave of agony.

"We can hold it," Rosemary said fiercely, though she wanted to scream instead.

It seemed interminable, the length of time they stayed locked together, bearing the tides of pain. But they stood strong, hands still clasped, enduring the force of physical anguish.

"Who is there?" a voice called out to them.

A figure moved faintly in the dimness, the wavering shape of a young man.

"Cucuc," Jimmy whispered. "It's me. We're here with you."

"You do this for me?" echoed the voice. "Then I shall stay, friends, to deliver you from this suffering."

"Do not break!" the Druid urged Rosemary and Jimmy. "Hold for the last and it will be easier for him."

Even as he spoke, the final flood of pain coursed through them, rushing to every part of their bodies like fire, till they could not help crying out.

They didn't break. They withstood it, and like the tide ebbing, the pain slowly withdrew, leaving them sobbing and weak with relief. The three separated. Rosemary held onto herself as the last edges of pain left her. Still shaking, Jimmy ran to Cuculann. The warrior was moaning, and moving slightly as if waking from sleep. His eyes fluttered and then opened.

"Jim," Cuculann said softly. "The pain is gone. I had a dream that you took it away."

Jimmy was laughing and crying, "We did it! We did it! He's okay!" he cried to Rosemary. "He's all right!"

Rosemary was laughing too, as the tears flowed down her face.

"We did it!" she cried, but when she turned to the Druid, she saw that he was unable to move. He was bent over and his face was ashen.

"You took the worst of it," she said anxiously, trying to hold him up.

"I will recover," he said weakly. "But I must leave you for a while. I must take another form."

"Do it then," Rosemary said. "You don't have to keep your promise after what you did. Come back to us when you're ready."

The change was so quick, she didn't see it. One moment she was holding the Druid steady, and the next, a tiny bird rested in the palm of her hand.

"Come back to us when you're ready," she said again, and she lifted up her hand to let the bird fly into the sky.

Jimmy had already helped Cuculann to his feet and the warrior was shouting and laughing because he felt so well. He gave Jimmy a big hug and then looked over at Rosemary who was watching them shyly.

"This pretty woman is your sister, James?"

He did not look so terrible after all, Rosemary thought, and she smiled when he kissed her on the cheek.

"I'll cook you some supper," Jimmy offered, as Cuculann rubbed his stomach and stretched. "I bet you're starving."

"So you have learned this skill at last!" Cuculann said happily, giving him a slap on the back. "Ah, but it is good to have company again!"

They sat around the fire and finished the stew that Jimmy had prepared. Cuculann made jokes about it as he ate, but he helped himself to many servings and belched appreciatively.

"Tell us what's been happening, Cucuc," Jimmy said eagerly. "Where are we and where are the armies?"

"This is the gravemound of Lerga on my own dear land, Muirthemne, and they, foul enemies, are camped at Breslech Mor on the plain. On my ground! My soil! They have captured the Brown Bull and sent it southwards with their plunder. I could not stop them, I was so weak with my wounds." Cuculann's shoulders sagged with weariness. "I have not slept for many nights and days. There have been countless combats and ambushes. Though I am healed now, I still have little strength."

"The armies are retreating then," Rosemary said to comfort him. "If they've got the bull and are moving south, they must be going home."

Cuculann's mouth tightened. "They will have to pay for this theft and the pillaging of our land. They will not reach Connaught before feeling the wrath of the men of Ulster."

"They've arisen?" Jimmy said.

"Not yet, but it will be soon. Then the last battle of the Tain will take place."

Cuculann's eyes closed and they watched with pity as he fought to open them again.

"You must sleep a while," Rosemary urged.

He smiled and shook his head. "I cannot lie here unguarded. It would be foolish. They will return to make certain I am dead."

Jimmy's face flushed. "You insult me, Cucuc. Wasn't I your charioteer? Don't I carry arms? Do you think I'm not good enough to defend you?"

Rosemary was proud of her brother and she agreed with him. He knew how to fight and she, well, she could learn. She wasn't afraid of death. She had faced it once already. Remembering that, her determination hardened.

"Yes Cucuc! —may I call you that too? —We can guard you while you rest."

Cuculann looked at their eager faces and though he hesitated at first, he finally consented to lie down for a short while. He had no sooner put his head to the ground than he was fast asleep. Jimmy grinned and Rosemary gently placed a blanket over the sleeping warrior. She brushed the hair from his eyes and he smiled in his sleep.

"Poor young man," she murmured. "You don't live an easy life, that's for sure."

"It's you and me now, Ro," Jimmy said and they smiled at each other fondly. "I'll teach you how to drive the chariot and I think you should learn some sword fighting as well. There isn't much time, but the more you know the better for both of us. Are you too tired to do it now?"

"Not really," she shrugged. "After all, it's not really night-time for us, is it?"

"Who knows?" he laughed. "This has to be the craziest jet-lag yet."

They rummaged through Cuculann's store of weapons till they found a sword that was suitable for Rosemary. It was the length of her arm but light and slim and when she bent it against the ground the point sprang back like a bowstring.

"Perfect," said Jimmy. "Now for a scabbard. I think you should use a wooden one. They're lighter than the bronze."

"It's still too heavy," she said, as the weight bent her forward.

Jimmy searched through the pile again, tossing articles aside till he found what he wanted.

"Here we go. Just the thing. Your shoulders will be stronger than your waist."

He strapped the leather baldric over her shoulder and the sword and scabbard hung down the side of her body.

"Much better," she said with relief.

They practised sword fighting together, Jimmy showing his sister how to hold the sword and lunge and parry.

"Watch your stance!" he yelled, as she fell backwards trying to evade him. "One foot in front of the other. Shoulder's width apart. You must keep your balance. If you fall down, you're done for."

They fought till their arms were tired and Rosemary begged for a rest. Remembering his gruelling training-in-arms in the Ulster camp, Jimmy shook his head with worry.

"There just isn't enough time, Ro. You need much more practice and your arms have to build up strength. The best plan is to make you charioteer and leave most of the fighting to me. But whatever happens, we've got to stick together. Now let's go for a run in the chariot."

Rosemary nodded tiredly. It certainly wasn't going to be as easy as she thought.

Cuculann's steeds whinnied in friendship as Jimmy yoked them to the chariot. He sat on the bench as his sister took up the reins nervously. For a moment Jimmy thought it funny to change places of teacher and pupil, but then he remembered that this was no joke. They would need every bit of skill and knowledge they could scrape together. He instructed Rosemary slowly and carefully.

"You'll have to hold the reins with one hand, the goad in the other. Lean back and don't slacken your grip. They'll think you're letting them run free if you do. Further back. That's it. Don't be upset by the noise. These things hold together no matter how fast you go or how many bumps you hit. Let's go!"

They rode into the night, the cool air tearing through them as Rosemary urged the horses to faster and faster paces. They turned the hill in a great roar, tearing up bushes and stones as the wheels bounced off the uneven ground. The chariot clattered as if it would burst asunder.

"You've got it!" Jimmy yelled, holding tightly to the bench.

Frightened and exhilarated, Rosemary fought for mastery over the great steeds. She grew accustomed to the rattle of the chariot and the insistent tugging at the end of the reins, and she circled the hill again and again. When they halted for a rest, she leaned breathlessly against the car, her eyes shining and her hair falling in her face.

"I wish I'd learned this sooner. It's fantastic!"

Jimmy laughed and was about to continue his instructions when his face paled.

"Look! Do you see it?" he hissed. "Something moving on the side of the hill, over there."

Her heart pounded as she searched through the darkness and found what he was pointing at; a dim figure creeping slowly towards their campsite.

"They're coming back to kill him," she said bitterly.

"So they think," her brother said in a grim voice. "Stay here till I call you."

"No way, charlie, we're in this together. You said I needed more practice."

Swords drawn, they crawled cautiously up the hill till they were a short distance from the intruder. With a sudden burst they ran at him, then stopped with relief.

The Druid looked down at them wryly.

"I could have killed you by now. A simple spear cast would have done it. I could see your swords shining like torches all the way up the hill. You are the easiest target, Rose," he said, pointing to her white sweater. "Go and change into one of Cuculann's tunics. Jimmy, bring up the chariot."

When they gathered at the campfire, the two had lost their confident air. They felt embarrassed and foolish, and they avoided the Druid's steady gaze.

"Do not lose heart," he said kindly. "I have been watch-

ing you. You are doing well. Remember this: never draw
your weapons at night till you are ready to strike, blacken
your faces with ash before you move out, and above all,
never become over-confident. In battle, that is the moment
when you die."

They nodded dumbly.

"I can protect you in a limited way as you are bound to
me in magic, but I do not have the power to make you
invincible. Your death could as likely occur here as elsewhere. You brought this upon yourselves by offering to be
Cuculann's guards."

This was met with a long silence.

"I'm ready to take the chance for Cuculann's sake,"
Jimmy said finally.

"Me too," Rosemary said in a low voice. "We're not just
fooling around. We know it's dangerous, and if it means
dying…"

"That may not be necessary," the Druid said. "I can cast
certain spells over you. The greatest is that you cannot be
killed as long as you do not kill."

They both brightened at this.

"Suits us fine," Jimmy said happily. "I don't think Ro
wants to kill and I know I don't. It may be the way of life
here, but I couldn't go home with blood on my hands."

"Really, it would be murder as far as we're concerned,"
his sister added.

"Then that is the shelter you will receive. This is not an
easy thing, I warn you. You will find it simpler to kill than
not to. You must watch every stroke you wield, every cast
you make, and in like turn, you can suffer the same wounds
you give."

"Sounds fair," they said.

"I will help you if you need me," he added. "Rest now. You have given Cuculann the gift of sleep and he has great need of it. He will not be with you for some time. When you are to take up your duties, I will call you."

Jimmy was asleep as soon as he curled up under his blanket, but Rosemary lay awake watching the Druid as he sat motionless by the fire. After a while she got up to join him.

"Are you better now?" she asked.

He smiled briefly at her concern. "It was not the pain that overcame me, but the use of my power. I had never directed it towards healing, and what is new can be shattering. The knowledge was good, however, and once again I must thank you for leading me to it."

"Oh you're welcome," Rosemary said easily.

She hugged her knees to her chin, and stared into the fire.

"You know, Peadar," she said softly, "until today, until we saved Cuculann, I never knew there was anything else besides the body. I know you told me that Druids' souls go from one form to another, but it didn't really mean anything to me. I mean, I never thought that *I* might have one." She smiled to herself. "I like it. I like having a soul."

Chapter Twenty-One

t was late morning when the Druid woke Rosemary and Jimmy.

"The time has come," he told them, as they ate their breakfast. "A young warrior troop is riding this way, the youth of Ulster who are not under the curse of the goddess Macha. One hundred and fifty of them ride to attack the Connaught armies."

Jimmy jumped up. "We'll go with them!"

Rosemary gulped her food. This was it. At least they wouldn't have to fight alone.

Peter had laid out battle-clothes and they dressed themselves in overcoats of hard leather, breastplates and helmets. Jimmy lifted his heavy, iron sword and the sunlight gleamed along its edges. He remembered the day Fergus gave it to him in exchange for the blunt training sword.

"You are ready for a warrior's weapon," Fergus had said.

"I sure hope he's right," Jimmy muttered now.

Rosemary strapped the leather baldric over her shoulder and looked doubtfully at the long, sharp sword she was to use. With a sudden thought of Maine, she tucked her own tiny dagger into the scabbard, and felt better.

"It's your first fight, sis," Jimmy said to her shyly. "Good luck kid," and they hugged each other.

As they mounted the chariot, Cuculann suddenly sat up in his sleep and cried out in a hollow voice.

"I summon the waters, the air and the earth. I call upon the gods of my people. Fare you well in battle, friends!"

He fell back unconscious and they stared at him in surprise. But the Druid looked pleased.

"As a son of the Sidhe he has placed a blessing on you as great as mine. Do not fear. You will do well."

With a great cry, Rosemary lashed at the horses and they sped from the gravemound of Lerga towards the northlands. They drove for miles at breakneck speed, scanning the hills for sight of the troop from Ulster. When they spotted a thin, dark line against the horizon, Jimmy shouted over the noise of the chariot.

"Circle to the right when they get close, to show we're friends!"

The troop was moving swiftly over the hills and Rosemary drew up the chariot in a field directly in their path. As the first Ulster cars drove into view, she circled to the right.

In the brilliance of the morning sun, the young company shone like a bright parade. Banners fluttered high and coloured plumes waved from the horses' bridles. Gold, silver and bronze flashed like fireworks. As the splendid band halted before them, one car broke from the rest to meet Rosemary and Jimmy. It was painted in royal purple and emblazoned with red and gold designs. The charioteer was a tiny girl no more than ten or twelve, but the youth beside her was a young warrior, and by his bearing, a prince and leader.

"Who are you, dark-haired ones?" he demanded.

He held a spear in his hand and his voice was cold and haughty.

Jimmy drew himself up, sensing the importance of the occasion. "We are James and Rosemary, son and daughter of Redding," he said. "We are the companions of the great Hound of Ulster and we ride under his blessing."

The prince's face changed at these words and the girl-charioteer laughed and tugged at his arm. She drew the car nearer till the wheels of both chariots were touching.

"I am Follamain," the prince said, putting his hand on Jimmy's shoulder. "I am the son of Conchobor, King of Ulster. This is my sister Cliodhna. I bring with me the youth-troop of Ulster to join our friend and comrade Cuculann in his fight against the provinces of Ireland."

Jimmy grasped Follamain's arm. "Cuculann is resting from his wounds. He has fought many battles and is ill and weak. But we'd like to ride with you if we can. The Connaught army is not far from here, at Breslech Mor on the Plain of Murtheimne."

"The companions of the Hound are welcome in my company," Follamain said and he pointed them a position to take in the troop.

Rosemary wheeled the chariot into place as the warriors waved and called out to her. She looked over the hosting of girls and young men, all slim and tall with yellow hair shining. Coloured cloaks twinkled in the sunlight and young faces laughed and shouted. They were the pride of Ulster. The sons and daughters of kings and chieftains.

"This is great, Jim," Rosemary said. "We belong here."

"Nothing like being in the thick of things," her brother agreed.

There was little order and great excitement as the troop resumed its jubilant drive towards the armies of Connaught. They crashed recklessly over field and valley, shouting their war cries and singing to the sky.

They did not have far to journey. Scouts had reported their movements and an armed force met them at Lia Toll.

Jimmy let out a yell and began casting spears from the chariot.

"Here we go," Rosemary muttered.

"Into the midst of them!" Jimmy shouted. "Don't stop for anything!"

She lashed at the horses till they were galloping madly onto the battlefield. The din was terrible: men shouting, horses squealing, metal clashing. Chariots crashed against each other with great, loud smacks. Spears whistled through the air. Patches of blood bloomed like dark flowers as the fighters hacked and hewed. The wounded screamed. The dying fell.

"Be careful, Jim!" Rosemary yelled, as her brother's spear sank into a warrior's side. The man fell from his chariot, blood gushing from the wound. "Oh please don't let it be fatal," she prayed.

She had little time to worry. A soldier was running at her from the side of the chariot and she drew her sword to defend herself.

"I must not kill. I must not kill," she repeated, as she parried his blows. But Peadar was right. It would be much easier if she could just lunge into him. She had the advantage from her height in the battle-car.

Her attacker was suddenly caught off balance by the press of men around him and seeing her chance, Rosemary brought the flat of her sword down upon his head. He fell to the ground unconscious, but she was certain he wasn't dead. More ran to take his place and she held her sword with two hands to beat them back. She cut and slashed and waved her sword before her in wide, sweeping arcs. Screams of pain rang in her ears whenever she landed a blow and she wondered how long she could keep going without fainting from fear and disgust. Her arms were already sore and sweat poured from her body. Another bore down on her, his wooden shield held before him like a battering ram. She lunged forward and with a cry of fright and anger, found that she couldn't pull free. She let go and her sword hung like a captive on the shield of her attacker. Jimmy heard her shouts and turned to defend her.

"Move back!" he cried. "Turn the chariot!"

She gathered the reins in both hands and pulled with all her might. The car turned slowly as the horses pushed against the throng. A path began to clear before them, and warriors jumped quickly to avoid the fierce trample of the hooves. But she was turning too fast. The horses faltered and stumbled. With a horrible crunching and upheaval, the chariot turned over. Rosemary and Jimmy were thrown to the ground, their store of weapons spilling around them. Before the mob closed in, they scrambled painfully to their feet. Jimmy grabbed his sword and shield, but Rosemary was too far from her weapons. Forcing down waves of terror, she drew her dagger and prepared to defend herself to the death.

"Will you kill me with my own gift?" a great cry reached her.

She looked up to find that she was about to fight Maine. His face was flushed with the heat of battle and his eyes blazed with fury. She looked frantically for Jimmy, but he had been beaten back to the Ulster lines and his shield blocked out her plight. She was surrounded by Connaughtmen and Maine's sword hovered above her head.

"Will you kill me with the arm that once held me?" she cried back.

He pulled her towards him, shouting at his men to give way and dragged her from the battlefield to a wooded hill nearby.

"I see you have joined my enemies with no pain in your heart for me!" he shouted, anger livid in his face.

"I was hardly treated with love the last time I was in your camp," she retorted and they glared at each other.

Then Maine smiled with sudden humour.

"For all that you hate her, you look very like my mother right now."

"Thanks a lot!" she said, but she couldn't help laughing.

They regarded each other fondly.

"I see you haven't exactly missed me," she said with a grin. "You look well."

"And you as pretty as ever, though fiercer now I think."

He bent over to kiss her.

"It's warring you should be at, son of Maeve, not love-making," a voice said angrily. Fergus strode up to them with Jimmy at his side. "I took this young pup from the fray before he met an untimely death at the hands of my men. I see you have done the same with the maiden, for reasons other than comradeship."

Fergus glowered at the Connaughtman, but Rosemary spoke up quickly.

"He is my…" she faltered and blushed under the old soldier's gaze, "my friend," she finished lamely. "He saved my life."

"Well, your 'friend' and I must return to the battle," Fergus said drily, "before we blacken our names as runaways. You and James will stay here. You have played your part for Cuculann's sake." Fergus's face paled and he put his hand to his brow. "But the young of Ulster will all be killed shortly and it is not your place to be included in the tragedy."

"What do you mean?" they cried.

Fergus refused to say more, and the two warriors returned to the field, leaving Rosemary and Jimmy to watch the end of the battle from their hilltop. At first, Rosemary kept her eyes on Maine, all her anxiety centering on where and how he was fighting. But as she began to realize the tide the battle was taking, her attention turned back to the youth-troop.

"Oh no," Jimmy said, with sick horror, "it can't be happening."

Only now did they realize that the youth-troop was hopelessly outnumbered. The gallant bravery of the young and the first splendid surge of the attack blinded them to the reality of the situation. The battle had been a joke to the Connaughtmen. Most stood on the sidelines and watched, till their leaders tired of the sport and ordered a full scale attack. In shock and disbelief, Rosemary and Jimmy saw the Connaughtmen surround each chariot and butcher the youngsters. Rosemary screamed in fury at the warriors who laughed as they slew their helpless foe. Jimmy wept with the Ulster exiles who carried out their terrible duty with faces grim and eyes wet with tears.

The young did not turn back. It was against their code of life. But they cried like the children they were as their friends died around them. There was no mercy or relief and they continued fighting in despair. One by one they fell till only Follamain and Cliodhna remained, the prince holding his shield before his sister as they fought together. Then they too fell to the bloodstained earth.

The armies withdrew, the Connaughtmen caterwauling their victory over the children of Ulster. Darkness fell over the land as the sun hid its golden face in horror, and the dimness of extinguished life settled over the broken bodies of the young. Rosemary and Jimmy wandered down to the field in a daze, stepping over the bodies and weeping out loud. They pulled their chariot upright and collected their weapons. The horses were grazing peacefully, oblivious to the carnage around them.

"It's not fair!" Rosemary screamed over the battlefield.

The only answer was the cry of carrion birds circling overhead. Jimmy pulled her into the chariot and they drove back to the gravemound of Lerga. The Druid looked at them sadly as they sat holding each other before the fire.

"You know now that war is no glorious game," he said quietly. "You see who suffers for it."

"How can this happen?" Rosemary asked dully.

Peter sighed. "That would be impossible for me to answer. There is no sensible explanation. But do not blame these people without remembering that it is also happening in your world and on a far greater scale."

"Yes, and for the same stupid reasons with the same stupid results," she said fiercely.

Rosemary buried her face in her hands. Jimmy stared

blindly into the fire. As the Druid began to chant, they both fell quietly into a deep and dreamless sleep. They did not wake till Cuculann himself shook them into consciousness.

Chapter Twenty-Two

uculann pushed and pummelled them and shouted in their ears. He stood over them all life and cheer, demanding that they rouse themselves and eat and talk with him.

"I am ready for a festival!" he cried happily. "For a long march!" He cocked his head towards Rosemary. "For making love all day!"

She shook her head and laughed at him.

While Jimmy and Cuculann went hunting, Rosemary gathered wood to build a fire. She looked around for the Druid but he had disappeared again. She remembered how gentle he had been when they returned from the battle.

"He's such a strange man," she thought. "Moody and mysterious," but she was beginning to like him.

As the three ate around the campfire, Cuculann was told of the rout of the Ulster youth.

"This would not have happened if I hadn't slept!" he cried.

"You would have died yourself if you didn't get some

rest," Jimmy argued, "and that wouldn't have helped matters any."

The warrior was hardly comforted. His face was dark and brooding.

"This very night I will attack the Connaught camp," he said fiercely. "I must avenge my brothers and sisters!"

He beat his fist upon the ground in grief and anger.

Jimmy looked at Rosemary anxiously. He didn't want Cuculann to go into a rage and frighten her.

"It'll be done tonight," Jimmy said, putting his hand on the warrior's arm, "and we will go with you. But in the meantime, why don't you relax and tell us a few stories. My sister knows very little about you, Cucuc."

The idea was a good one. Cuculann's worn face brightened when Rosemary said she would love to hear all about him. Jimmy handed around the gourd of ale as Cuculann began his story.

"I was born to Deicthne, sister of Conchobor. She was his charioteer in her youth, but when she came of age she married the warrior Sualdim. I call him 'father' though it is rightly known that my mother was bearing me before she wed; a child conceived when she swallowed a flea in her cup of wine."

At this remark Rosemary snickered despite her efforts not to. Cuculann looked at her bemused.

"It is a common enough occurrence. The gods pull these little tricks to give their children to mortal women. The Sidhe—they are the gods of our land—do this quite regularly," he said with a grin. "They have a peculiar liking for our women.

"My real father," he went on, "is Lug mac Ethenn, the warrior-god who carries the spear. It is he who gave me the gift of my battle fury. I cannot be bested when it explodes within me.

"My birth name was Setanta and I was reared at Forth Imrith in a great oaken house on my beloved plain of Murtheimne. When I was five years old, I heard of the youth-troop of Ulster: one hundred and fifty young comrades learning the crafts and arts of war in the court of the King. I yearned to join these and begged my mother to let me go.

"'You cannot go, little one,' she said to me, 'till the warriors come for you.'

"'I will not wait, Mother,' I said, 'I will die of loneliness without boys to fight and play with.'

"She hated to refuse me my heart's desire and she knew already that I would leave her some day. She sighed unhappily and agreed.

"'It is a long way for a boy-child to travel, but I know you would go without my blessing and I will not have that.'

"She told me to go northward and over the mountain of Sliab Fuait. I took up my toy shield and my hurling stick and ball, and set out on the road to Emain Macha, the court of the King. Though the way was long, no harm befell me. Days later, without sleep or stopping, I came upon the boys of the youth-troop as they played together in a field." Cuculann's eyes twinkled as he remembered. "There are rules of play among young warriors, but I was ignorant of them. I did not state my kinship or ask their pledge of safety and they attacked me." He started laughing, "Oh, I was so mad! I knocked them about—black eyes and broken noses,

skinned elbows and knees! I piled them in a heap, so furious
was I that they would attack one of their own."

"All of them?" Rosemary said incredulously.

"He could do it!" Jimmy said. "What happened after
you beat them up, Cucuc?"

"The ruckus and the uproar reached the halls of the
King and he rode out to discover the meaning of the
commotion. He was astonished to find all the lads moaning
and groaning and pointing to me as the cause.

"'These boys have been badly treated,' Conchobor said
sternly.

"I stood my ground.

"'I am not wrong, Uncle,' I said, 'I journeyed far to join
them and they attacked me first.'

"'Did you not ask for their protection before you came
onto the playing field?' he demanded, and I realized my
error.

"'I didn't know I had to ask such a thing," I replied, 'but
I will give them my oath now if they give me their's.'

"The King was pleased to see me as he knew who I was.
He had the boys shake hands with me and all was forgotten
in new friendship."

Cuculann smiled sadly. They could see the anguish in his
eyes before he bowed his head.

"All dead now," he whispered.

"If your name was Setanta," Rosemary said quickly,
"why are you called 'Cuculann'?"

The warrior trembled visibly as he fought to control his
feelings.

"There are two stories to my name," he said at last. "The
first is how I came to be at the King's right hand.

"When I was but six years of age and still without weapons, Eoghan Mac Durthact, the black king of Fernmag, invaded our land. The warriors rode out to meet him, but it was an evil day for Ulster. Our men were defeated, and Mac Durthact left victorious, driving his plunder of cattle before him. None of the Ulstermen returned and the King was believed to be dead. The youth-troop took counsel that night and decided to wait till morning to recover the bodies of the slain; for it is in the dark of night that the goddess of slaughter, the Badb, runs madly through the corpses of war.

"I who have feared neither man nor god set out that very night to see if my uncle were alive or dead. I played my hurling stick around the spattered battlefield, bashing the heads of the fallen men of Fernmag. Then a green and horrible vision came to me, the red mouth of the Badb as she devoured the dead."

"Yechhh," said Rosemary and Jimmy.

Cuculann shrugged. "No man who carries the name 'warrior' should be bothered by ghosts. I ignored her.

"I soon reached the heart of the field where the Ulster dead lay thickest. Here I would find the King, I knew, for to the last man they had defended him. I heard a feeble moan and my eyes hunted through the darkness till I found him. He was broken and bleeding, but with life still in him.

"'Is Conchobor to be found here?' I called out.

"He roused himself at the sound of my voice.

"'Why came you here, son,' he said, grimacing with pain. 'Do you wish to know the meaning of death?'

"I threw off the bodies of his men where they had died around him, and I carried him from the field. A warm fire and roast meat helped to bring back his strength and together we searched for his eldest son and found him alive. I fed and nursed the two till they were able to return to Emain Macha."

"So the King owes you his life and his son's," Jimmy said proudly.

Cuculann laughed. "The King owes nothing to me or anyone else, just as I owe nothing to him unless I choose."

"Don't you swear allegiance to him?" Rosemary asked, but she suddenly remembered Fergus and the Ulster exiles.

As if he knew her mind, Cuculann echoed the old warrior's words, "Nothing binds a warrior save his own honour. We defend our land and people, but only because we choose to. We are bound only to our name and honour.

"But though the King was not indebted to me for saving him, he came to love me as his favourite above all others. When he was invited to feast or festival, he took me with him just as he brought his closest counsellors, Druids, and chieftains. It was at such an invitation that I received my name of manhood.

"Culann the Smith, the greatest craftsman of Ulster, held a feast one day for the King and his court. As Conchobor rode out to Culann's house, he came upon the youth-troop playing their games in a field. He called out to me to ride with him, but when I play a game I like to finish, and I shouted back that I would follow later.

"The day was warm and sunny and the King was full of cheer as he looked forward to the food and ale that Culann would lay before him. When he arrived at the Smith's fort, he was asked if there were more guests to come. Conchobor forgot his words with me and answered 'nay'.

"'Then I shall release the guardian of my land,' Culann said, 'the greatest hound in all Ireland. He is a beast that no man can fight without dying.'

"The King and his men were soon enjoying themselves. There were harpers, dancers, poets and acrobats. Black ale flowed freely from the Smith's huge vat and scores of deer, pigs, and cattle were slaughtered for the feast.

"In the meantime my game was completed and I took up my hurling stick and ball and set out on the road to Culann's. I had only stepped one foot upon his land when a bayful roar sounded over the hills. Before I could move, the great hound came rushing down upon me. He was of massive size, snow-white, with eyes as red as blood. His jaws opened like a great cavern to swallow me. I threw my hurling ball with such force that it crashed through his throat, yet still he ran, lashing out with his terrible paws to beat me into the ground. Now to die at the hands of a man is a noble death, but to be killed by a beast is the worst of shames. I knew that my honour demanded me to live. I rose up from my wounds and struck him again and again with my hurling stick. I must have hit him a hundred times before he lay quiet at my feet.

"The dying howls of the great hound sounded in Culann's hall and the Smith and the King rode out to meet the intruder. It was only when Conchobor saw me that he remembered his invitation. He was so delighted to see me alive that he tossed me into the air and held me in his arms.

"'I am glad to see that your young nephew has survived my hound,' Culann said sadly to the king, 'but this is an evil day for me. I shall not find the likes of that beast again and my land will fall to ruin and plunder without its guardian.'

"I understood his plight and spoke up quickly.

"'Do not mourn great Smith,' I said. 'I shall train a hound from the same litter and till he is fit to guard your borders, I shall do so myself.'

"Though I was but a child, the Smith had heard of my prowess and he was content and happy with my words.

"'You have taken on the first duties of manhood,' the King said proudly. 'You will be named 'Cuculann', the Hound of Culann, and you will be known in this land as the Great Hound of Ulster.'"

"Wonderful!" Rosemary said, clapping her hands, "and now you guard the borders of Ulster as well!"

Cuculann looked pleased with her outburst, but it returned him abruptly to the present. He walked moodily to the edge of the hill. In the distance the smoke of the Connaught campfires sullied the sky. He shook his fist angrily in their direction.

"When the sun sets we shall strike," he told them. "Jim, you must lay out my battle-dress, all my weapons, and the sickle-harness of the chariot. Hone and shine every piece. Make repairs where needed. Can you do this alone?"

"Of course I can. Fergus taught me all that in my training."

"Maiden," Cuculann said, turning to Rosemary. "I dreamed you handled a chariot and proved fearless in battle. My mother was the King's charioteer. I would have you be mine."

"But... but what about Jim?" she asked, embarrassed.

Cuculann smiled proudly as he put his hand on Jimmy's shoulder.

"I dreamed also that my dear friend was a full-fledged warrior. He will fight by my side."

Jimmy's face reddened, but his eyes shone.

"In that case, I'd be honoured," Rosemary said happily.

Cuculann's smile broadened. "You have a way that reminds me of my own Emer. It is better for a woman to have strength than beauty, but it is better still when she has both."

Rosemary blushed and thought to herself that she had never received so great a compliment.

"We will drive down to the sea and back," the warrior said, as they mounted the chariot.

"Lead on MacDuff," Rosemary said, and at his puzzled look she laughed, "Never mind, Cucuc, it would take too long to explain."

Chapter
Twenty-Three

hen Rosemary and Cuculann returned from their practice-run, Jimmy proudly showed them his handiwork. Bundles of clothes lay neatly folded on the grass, each with a helmet perched on top. The weapons were stacked against each other, carefully grouped by size and metal. There were short, bronze swords, thick and blunt for stabbing; long, graceful iron swords, sharp from hilt to point, for hewing and thrusting; and numerous scabbards and sheaths, some plain, some adorned with jewels and precious metals. The polished shields lay on the ground like huge, shining plates. Some were round like the sun and fashioned from copper, bronze, and iron; others were triangular in shape, carved from a single piece of black alderwood and covered in leather. The spears stood butt-end to the ground, their grey tips glinting at the sky. Daggers, darts, stones and slings lay loosely in piles to be chosen from at random.

Cuculann wandered through the display inspecting everything closely. "Well done," was all he said, but his tone repaid Jimmy for his labours.

"You will be dressed first, charioteer," Cuculann said to Rosemary as he handed her one of the bundles.

For a few awkward moments he stood looking at her expectantly. Jimmy saw what was wrong and grinned.

"Well I'm not going to get dressed right in front of you!" Rosemary finally said, and she blushed furiously.

"But why do you hide your body?" Cuculann asked astonished.

"I have no intentions of getting involved in that discussion at all," she said in a huff. "You can tell me where and how these things go on and I'll change in the bushes."

Barely suppressing his laughter, the warrior explained the nature of the battleclothes and Rosemary hurried into the cover of the trees, ignoring the howls of the two boys.

"And both of you get dressed before I come out!" she yelled back. "I'm not interested in any of your attributes either."

Cuculann stripped naked and dressed with Jimmy's assistance. His tunic was of waxed skin, pleated and pressed in a hundred tiny folds and tied with strings and straps at the side. Over this he wore a leather belt studded with bronze knobs that covered his stomach and chest. Around his waist he tied a silken apron hemmed with gold, and around his shoulders he tossed a crimson cloak that swirled to his feet. The mantle was clasped under his chin by a great ivory brooch shaped in the head of a snarling hound. Jimmy chose the largest helmet crested with bright stones and designs in red gold and set it carefully on Cuculann's head.

"My weapons I choose myself," the warrior said, "as you must choose yours. We will clothe you now. What is your father, Jim?"

"A judge," the boy replied, not understanding the question.

"That is a noble profession. You may wear the silken apron."

Jimmy wasn't particularly concerned with his status, but he was happy to dress like his friend. When he was ready, he looked like another version of Cuculann.

"Now the sickle-harness, Jim. You have cleaned and repaired the parts? Good."

They gathered up the barbed, iron-plated harness which covered the horses from mane to tail so that they looked like giant porcupines. The wooden chariot-wheels were replaced with ones of bronze that were spiked and sharpened with long nails and sickle-heads. Every inch of the battle-car bristled with points for tearing and ripping. The horses tossed their heads and pawed the ground impatiently. They knew the weight of the war-harness and they could smell the blood of battle in the air.

"Your servants await you, proud Rose!" Cuculann called to the bushes.

As Rosemary stepped into view, the boys whistled with admiration. She was a slender girl and her height was accented by the formal dress of war. A short red tunic fell lightly to her knees and her slim legs were crisscrossed with the straps of her sandals. She wore the deerskin coat of the charioteer, bared at the arms for freer movement, and a feathered cape that swept down her back. She had piled her dark hair under a silver helmet that curved down the nape of her neck and around her ears in spirals.

Cuculann painted a circle of ochre on her brow.

"The sign of my charioteer," he said. "If I lose you in battle I will look for that mark."

Rosemary and Jimmy stood ready before Cuculann. He put his hands on their shoulders and smiled.

"No man could ask more of his friends than that they would be willing to die with him. Of all the gifts that the gods have given me, I thank them most heartily for this."

They had hard lumps in their throats, but they held their heads proudly.

Even as they smiled back at him, the warrior's face began to change. His eyes glazed over and when he spoke again, his voice was incredibly loud and deep.

"Do not fear what is coming over me, friends. My love for you will protect you. But WOE TO MINE ENEMIES!"

The last cried in a deafening roar, he broke away from them and began to shudder in great, violent spasms. He raised his arms to the sky and his entire body expanded, pressing against his clothing as if the blood boiled beneath his skin. His eyes rolled white in his head and he let out a terrible scream. The muscles of his legs knotted and bulged, and he stamped the ground with furious crashes. They watched in horror as black smoke curled around his head and flashes of fire burst here and there around him.

"To the chariot!" Jimmy shouted. "If we don't get him to battle he will kill us, no matter what he says!"

Rosemary fought down the primeval terror that was overcoming her and she ran to the chariot with Cuculann close behind. She seized the reins and lashed at the horses till they were speeding towards the Connaught armies.

They came in sight of the camp as the sun completed its

burning descent into the hills. The sky and the earth were
bathed in a blood-red glow and Rosemary wondered for a
moment if it wasn't some terrible omen. But she had little
time to think. Cuculann was roaring his orders and she
drove full tilt into the centre of the camp.

Cuculann's ferocious war cries threw all into surprise
and confusion. The bristling battle-car plowed through
tents, chariots, and stores of weapons till debris littered the
ground. If a person or animal came in her path, Rosemary
swerved madly to knock them over without tearing them to
pieces on the sickle-harness. On either side of her, Jimmy
and Cuculann fought off anyone who recovered enough to
fight back, but while Cuculann slew all who came near him,
Jimmy used the flat of his weapon only. As they tore
violently through the crowd, Rosemary spotted the Queen's
tent a short distance away. On a sudden impulse, she pulled
the horses round and smashed through the royal quarters,
laughing loudly as the sharp barbs ripped everything to
shreds.

"If only Maeve was inside!" Rosemary shouted, when
they cleared the rubble. Her face was unnaturally bright
and her eyes glowed wildly.

Jimmy pulled at her arm and his shocked look cooled her
down. Cuculann only laughed.

"Out of the camp now, fierce beauty, before we are
swamped by these maggots!"

Completely unscathed and singing with triumph, they
sped from the camp as abruptly as they had arrived.

"They didn't know what hit them!" Jimmy cried, looking
back at the rampant confusion.

They drove on till they were certain no one was following.

Rosemary drew up the chariot near a sheltered ford on the River Fane.

"That was pretty heavy stuff on the Queen's tent," Jimmy said to his sister, when they had set up their camp. "I don't believe your temper sometimes."

"She had it coming—for one royal slap in the face," Rosemary said hotly, though she felt a little ashamed.

"Women," Jimmy said, winking at Cuculann.

But it was the warrior's turn to complain. He had been silent since they left the scene of their attack.

"You did not kill a single one," Cuculann said accusingly, looking at both sister and brother. "I saw this even in my battle fury."

Jimmy sighed and shrugged, "We can't kill, Cucuc. It's as simple as that."

"It's against the law where we come from," Rosemary added.

Cuculann stared hard at them as if to convince himself they were telling the truth.

"No one kills in your world?" he demanded, and his disbelief was evident.

Rosemary and Jimmy looked at each other.

"No one's supposed to," they said, and left it at that.

The next morning, as they were having breakfast, a chariot pulled up on the other side of the river.

"It's Fergus!" Jimmy said, in surprise. "He's not coming to challenge you, is he?"

Cuculann sighed, "He has been tricked by Maeve, no doubt. But he was my teacher and at one time my foster-father. Those bonds are sacred. I cannot and will not fight him."

Fergus walked to the edge of the ford and stood with his hands on his hips. Even across the river it was obvious that his scabbard was empty.

"You must be blessed by the gods, friend Fergus," Cuculann called out, "if you intend to fight me with no weapon."

The old warrior smiled fondly, "It wouldn't matter if I had a sword, Hound, I would not strike you. Give way for the sake of our friendship and let the armies cross this ford in my name."

Cuculann thought a moment. "Are you prepared to go under pact of truce on mutual terms?"

Fergus hesitated, then nodded abruptly. "I am. I will do anything rather than fight you, my son."

Cuculann spoke formally, "By the honour of truce and by our bond of fosterage, I yield to you now if you yield to me in future."

Fergus responded in the same tone, "By the honour of truce and by our bond of fosterage, I pledge to yield to you, once, upon your demand."

As they drove away from the ford Rosemary said to Cuculann, "You're very reasonable when you want to be."

"There are laws to govern such agreements," he replied with a shrug, "and I obey them. To break the pact of words is to bring chaos upon yourself and the world. But I am happy to make truce with Fergus, and it will free my beloved land of the foul presence of the Connaughtmen."

He gave her directions to turn west and travel upstream of the river.

"It's a good guess that the armies will halt at Crich Rois. We will camp at the bog of Fuiliarnn and keep an eye on them."

"This is spooky," Jimmy said as they settled down in the dark, black bog.

"It's flat," Cuculann said. "A good arena for the next bout of single combat. I will continue to challenge them as they move, to slow their progress. My appetite for Connaughtmen still rages."

It was not long before the armies caught up with them and once again Fergus arrived in his chariot. When Jimmy saw the old warrior's face, he knew something was terribly wrong.

"I have come to warn you of your next challenger," Fergus said to Cuculann.

"Only you could warn me of any man, Fergus, without dying for the insult. Who is he?"

"Your brother, Ferdia."

Chapter Twenty-Four

 won't fight him!" Cuculann cried, jumping up. "He is my best friend! My older brother! He saved my life a hundred times and I, his. This is treachery. This is a lie!"

Fergus shook his head gravely. "It is no lie, Hound, though it *is* treachery. Maeve's wiles, the promise of Finnabar, and the mockery of the satirists have led Ferdia to swear by your death. For your honour and your life you must fight him."

Cuculann's face contorted with emotion. He ran from them and crashed through the bog, tearing up bushes and hitting out at the trees. The three watched helplessly as he disappeared from sight.

"I didn't even know he had a brother," Jimmy said in a low voice.

"Ferdia is his foster-brother," Fergus said, "but to the warrior, fostership is the closest of bonds, greater even than that of flesh and blood. Foster-brothers are reared together like twins. They pledge loyalty and love to each other, defend and protect one another, and share all miseries and joys. This combat goes against the warrior's code and all that is right and sacred to us, but, nevertheless, Maeve's trickery has brought it about and Cuculann has no choice but to fight."

"Will they fight to kill?" Rosemary whispered.

"One or both will surely die when they meet. They are the two greatest warriors in Ireland, each learned in the same crafts and skills, each aware of the other's strengths and weaknesses."

"I don't like the sound of this," Jimmy said. "We can't be of much help if Ferdia is as good as Cuculann." He looked in the direction the warrior had fled and his voice sounded desperate, "Isn't there anything we can do?"

Perhaps there is," Fergus said thoughtfully. "They will be feteing Ferdia at the camp tonight with feast, women, and drink. A warrior ever loves to be coddled and pampered and it can affect his fighting spirits greatly. Cuculann should have like treatment. There is one person who can feast and pamper him to his tastes—his wife, Emer."

"We'll go for her," they said together.

"Not both of you. You may not return in time and Cuculann should not face this alone. James, you and I shall drive him to the Ford of Ardee where the combat is to take place. You must stay by him. He will need you to prepare and encourage him. Rosemary can take the chariot and I will give her instructions where and how to find Dun Delga, Cuculann's fort."

Jimmy frowned. He had sworn to himself that he wouldn't be separated from his sister. Rosemary guessed his thoughts and spoke up quickly.

"It's all right by me, Jim. If we have to do it this way,

then we will. You came back here for Cuculann's sake and
he needs you more than ever now. Anyway, I'll be in the
safest position. The horses are fast and I won't stop till I
reach Dun Delga. But what about you? If Cucuc is killed..."

"He can't be killed," Jimmy said flatly, but he sounded
uncertain. Fergus's anxiety was affecting the two of them.

Rosemary looked around her. "Peadar, wherever you
are, if you can hear me, please stay with my brother. I'll be
fine."

With her weapons close at hand, Rosemary set out at
twilight to find Dun Delga. She drove at high speed through
the dusky evening, her eyes and ears intent on the sights and
sounds of the countryside. As the darkness deepened she was
guided by the stars and the shadows of the great mountains.
The swift galloping of the horses reassured her and her fears
of ambush were quieted by the silence and emptiness of the
night. As morning dawned to cheer and encourage her, she
came in sight of the fort that Fergus had described.

Set on a high, grassy mound that commanded a view of
the entire plain, Dun Delga showed little of itself to outsiders.
A tall, wooden palisade encircled the hill fort and only the
rising smoke of campfires told Rosemary that someone lived
within. She drove up to the gate and hammered against it
with the butt of her spear.

"Hold still!" a woman's voice eventually sounded from
within.

A young girl appeared on the ramparts. She pointed a
long spear at Rosemary and her beautiful face was hard and
suspicious.

"Who are you?" she demanded. "And why do you drive
my husband's chariot?"

Rosemary smiled a moment. The fierce voice was almost an echo of Cuculann's, but the yellow, ribboned braids and the warm, brown eyes were those of a lovely girl no older than herself.

"Are you Emer?" she said. "I am Rosemary Redding, friend to Cuculann. Please let me in to speak with you."

Emer hesitated, then called behind her, "Stand guard, Manus, only one."

She disappeared as the gate creaked open, and Rosemary drove into the courtyard of Dun Delga. A great wooden house fortified with stone dominated the compound. Around it stood smaller buildings of clay and thatch. Fires burned in the yard and chickens, goats and dogs wandered freely. Women and children stopped in their chores to stare at her as several armed men escorted her to the house. In the great hall, Emer stood waiting for her with arms folded in obvious dislike.

"And what kind of friend might you be to my husband?" she said archly.

Rosemary felt herself getting angry, but she didn't want to be blunt and upset the girl.

"My brother and I have been with Cuculann on the Tain. We are his charioteers and companions. Fergus mac Roich sent me with the message that your husband is in need of you."

Emer's coolness faded at these words.

"What is wrong with him?" she cried. "Is he dying?"

"No, no," Rosemary said quickly. "It's not that. He's to fight someone today, his foster-brother…"

"Not Ferdia! How could he? Cuculann loves him. This is madness. This cannot be true."

"It's one of Maeve's tricks," Rosemary said. "It's already

been settled. They were to begin at sunrise this morning."

Emer asked no more questions and moved quickly.

"Wait here while I gather a few things. We can take fresh horses and leave immediately."

Rosemary was left alone in the hall and a servant brought her food and hot wine. Tired and aching, she sat down on a bench and congratulated herself on the success of her mission.

"So this is Cucuc's home," she thought, looking around her.

There was an air of grandeur and power in the great, dark hall. The cavernous fireplace, now empty and silent, would burn whole logs to heat and light the room. The heavy beams of black oak and red yew were hung with woven cloths, weapons and the skins and heads of animals. The long wooden tables would seat a hundred or more and Rosemary imagined them crowded with loud, burly warriors shouting for meat and ale. Cuculann's wealth was obvious in the bright profusion of gold and jewelled ornaments scattered throughout the hall. It was a place that suited him, she decided.

Emer came hurrying back, dressed for travel.

"The chariot is ready. I have stocked it with everything my husband needs. You can tell me what has happened as we ride."

The return journey seemed much longer to Rosemary as she drove impatiently to reach her brother and Cuculann. Shouting over the rattle of the chariot, she told Emer the story of the Tain and how she and Jimmy had come to be the warrior's companions. When she was finished, Emer smiled at her shyly.

"I am shamefaced, Rose, for my cold welcome. Cucuc is

well liked by the women and I am often jealous of my own
kind. Now that I know what you and your brother have
done for him…"

"That's okay, forget about it. Friends?"

"Friends," Emer smiled.

They reached the ford past midday, but it was empty.
They looked with dismay at the bloodstained earth and the
signs of a fierce battle.

"It has already begun, perhaps over," Emer murmured,
and she threw back her head and cried out her husband's
name.

"Here you are at last!" a voice called out, and Jimmy
came running from the underbrush. "I've been waiting for
hours. You're Emer?"

"Cuculann?" she whispered.

Jimmy hesitated. "He's all right. He's hurt, but a Druid
is with him. We're on a hill not far from here."

When they arrived at the campsite they found the warrior
sprawled on a mat by the fire, half-conscious and moaning
with pain. Peter was leaning over him and bandaging his
wounds. As Emer ran towards them, Cuculann sat up
shakily and held out his arms.

"You did a great job, sis," Jimmy said, as he helped
Rosemary unyoke the horses.

"I'm really beat," she said, "but I want to hear about the
fight. What happened?"

They moved out of earshot and Rosemary collapsed on
the grass.

"Ferdia is built like Cucuc but bigger," Jimmy began.
"They went at it twice. The first time they hardly touched.
They danced around each other doing their feats—you

know, throwing spears and dodging them, stuff like that. The second time they charged at each other like bulls, shouting and striking till they drew blood. The river was red with it and the ground and grass. I was amazed that neither of them was killed."

"You mean Ferdia's still alive?!"

Jimmy nodded. "They'll go at it again tomorrow. It was pitiful, Ro, you wouldn't have been able to bear it. When they were finished they leaned against each other to hold themselves up. Cuculann kept putting his hands against Ferdia's wounds to stop the bleeding and Ferdia was doing the same back to him. They were still hugging each other when we pulled them apart to look after their wounds."

"Oh, why don't they call it off?"

"Impossible. It's a question of honour."

"Damn honour! What kind of honour makes you kill your friends?"

"It's what they believe in," he sighed.

"Well, I'm sick of it," she said furiously. "They do nothing but kill each other and make up songs and stories about it as if it's the most wonderful thing in the world. It's a pack of lies. You saw those kids die, Jim, and now Cuculann and his brother. It doesn't make any sense. All because of a stupid brown bull and honour. It's disgusting!"

Out of sheer frustration and weariness she started to cry. Jimmy put his arm around her and waited till she was finished.

"I couldn't agree with you more," was all he said.

"Ho, friends!" Cuculann called to them. "Come and join me. I sit like a chieftain in my hall!"

"Come on, Ro, put on a cheerful face," Jimmy said.

"We've got to see him through it, no matter what happens."

"I know," Rosemary said sadly, "but I really don't want him to die, Jim."

"Don't think about that," Jimmy urged. "It won't make things any easier."

Despite their gloom, they had to smile when they saw Emer's work.

There sat Cuculann in the midst of a lavish meal, beaming happily as Emer fed him from her hand. The feast was spread all around him to delight his eye and encourage his appetite. There were platters of lamb, crackling pork, brown beef and venison. Smoked fish lay wrapped in green leaves with periwinkles, prawns, and bright pink crabs. There were goblets of wine and gourds of black beer, tiers of pastries, cakes and fruits, and bowls of walnuts, sloes and cherries.

It was easy to forget the dangers of the coming day as they feasted late into the evening. Their loud laughter and chatter rose to the sky with the sparks of the bright campfire. When they grew tired they stretched out on their stomachs to watch the falling flames and their voices dropped to a companionable murmur. Emer took out her harp and strummed it quietly. Cuculann lay his head in her lap, as she sang to him in a high, gentle voice—

> "My treasure among men of the sun,
> My treasure among men of the mountain,
> You brought me to live in your Dun,
> You drenched me in your fountain.
>
> My gold, my cloths, my linen and my toys,
> What are these to me? Slash them with a knife,

You are my gold, my keepsakes, and joy,
You are my delight, my treasure, my life.

I will prepare you a feast,
With wine and roast meat,
I will make you a bed,
And lie at your head,
I will call the harper, the poet, and bard,
I will sing myself and while you sleep, keep guard.

My love and my sweetness!

I will wash your tunic white
And lay it on the bough to dry,
And I will envy its sight,
For against your breast it lies.

My love and my breath!

Dark, dark was my life
Till you took me from my father
To become your wife.

Golden man with weapons shining,
Like the sun, face as fair,
Ah, you set me pining
Man, tall as the spear!"

Emer sang through the night never stopping in her vigil over her husband. Looking up at the stars, Rosemary lay listening to the sad, sweet strains.

"Such a green country," she thought. "Why do they keep painting it red?"

Chapter Twenty-Five

he next morning Emer dressed Cuculann herself, taking care not to disturb the bandages that covered most of his body. The others moved around quietly, afraid to say or do anything that would hint at the danger ahead. Cuculann said little and kept looking in the direction of the battle-ford, but when he was ready he turned to his wife and kissed her on the eyes and mouth.

"I have strayed at times, Emer, but you know yourself that you are all and everything to me."

Her arms were around his neck and she swooned against him. When she stood back she was still trembling, but her voice was firm.

"Beloved, you are the breath I live by. Keep my name on your lips and you will come back to me."

Jimmy drew up the chariot and Cuculann joined him without looking back.

Emer turned to Rosemary. "I will stay here. If defeat and death are to come to him today, it is not my place to see it."

Rosemary nodded. There was nothing she could say to the girl, but she hugged her tightly before she left.

When they arrived at the ford, Ferdia and his charioteer were waiting for them. Ferdia stood a head taller than Cuculann and his build was thick and heavy. A full beard covered his broad, friendly face and laughter lines creased the corners of his eyes. But as he walked towards them, his body shuddered and he stooped like an old man. The shadow of suffering clouded his handsome features.

"Welcome, brother," he said to Cuculann.

Cuculann stood straight and refreshed before him.

"Once such words would have been in friendship and love, Ferdia, and I could freely give my hand to you. But it is I who should speak the welcomes. This is my land, my home, and you are the intruder here. You are in the wrong. Give up this quarrel."

Ferdia smiled wearily. He raised his arm and let it drop again.

"I will not argue today, Cucuc. My wounds kept me awake last night and I had much time to think. I am breaking our bond, the pledge we made to each other as children. We fought side by side and ate our meat from one plate. We hunted game and slept in the same bed in the forest. Together we learned about war and women and laughed long at each other's mistakes. But it is too late. I am entrapped. My honour would be destroyed if I turn aside now. This thing is done and we must finish it."

"It will finish you or me," Cuculann said sadly "Why have you done this Ferdia? Why? Had I been offered the woman or all the riches in the country, I would not have broken my oath with you. There is no one in the world, save Emer, for whom I would injure you, not father, mother, or comrade. Why have you done this?"

Ferdia shrugged his shoulders and his laugh was wistful.

"You know me well, Cucuc. I drink too much. I talk too much. I am always getting myself into trouble."

"And I always helped you out of it! But this is one mess, Ferdia, I cannot put right for you."

"Sweet brother," Ferdia sighed. "There is no greater warrior, no dearer friend in Ireland, that I could love. I know this is our undoing. Whoever wins today will win with sorrow. I pity us, friend, and it is to my shame that I have brought this upon us."

They embraced each other and broke apart. Ferdia turned to his charioteer and took up his weapons. Cuculann walked back to Jimmy, muttering and shaking his head. Jimmy could see the tears in his eyes.

"This will not be easy, James. This I dread more than anything I have ever faced. I have no desire for death and yet I do not wish to kill. Remember, you must encourage me. Mock me if I am failing so that my fury will be roused. Praise me if I am winning so that I will know the tide has turned for me."

Jimmy nodded and reached out to touch Cuculann but the warrior picked up his weapons and walked slowly back to the ford.

The two combatants circled each other warily. No words were spoken, but their quick breaths rasped the air. Then with great cries they attacked. Metal clashed as their swords met and giant blows rained upon their shields. They fought face to furious face, the rage of battle distorting their features till all love and friendship was obliterated. The grass around them darkened with their blood, as they struck each other with awesome and terrible force. Cries of pain rose with the howls of fury. They broke apart, covered in sweat and blood.

"We will fight in the river!" Cuculann cried.

They fell into the water, rolling and cursing and gripping each other by the throat. Cuculann climbed on Ferdia's shield to strike at his head, but Ferdia threw him off with a great thrust that knocked him onto the bank. Cuculann was dazed and slow to recover and Ferdia charged down upon him.

Jimmy bit his lip and ran to the edge of the river.

"You're an old dog, Hound of Ulster, a cur for the kennel! You are beaten. Run with your tail between your legs!"

Cuculann swelled with rage as the battle fury shook through his body. He stepped menacingly towards Jimmy, but Ferdia's charge cut him off and he turned to meet it with furious roars.

"It's a good thing for you that Ferdia was there," Rosemary said grimly to her brother.

"Just following orders," he said in the same tone, "and it worked. Now you're at your greatest, Hound!" he shouted again, "You are invincible! You are…"

His cries died in his throat and Rosemary screamed, as Cuculann staggered back from Ferdia. Blood poured from a deep gash in his chest and his eyes were half-mad. He cried out to Jimmy.

"The *gae-bolga*! Quick, friend, before I am finished!"

Jimmy dashed to the chariot and pulled out the secret weapon that the warrior had never let him touch. The round leather ball was small but heavy and Jimmy held it carefully as he ran back to the ford.

Cuculann dealt a hideous blow that struck Ferdia's shield from his hands.

"Now, friend!" he roared, and Jimmy threw the weapon.

With the last breath of his strength, Cuculann caught the gae-bolga and flung it furiously at his opponent. A terrible scream pierced the air as Ferdia clutched his stomach. The ball burst and hundreds of tiny barbs shot into his body, carrying poison to every part.

"That ends it, brother," Ferdia choked. "You have killed me with that," and he toppled backwards into the water.

Cuculann ran to Ferdia and despite his own great wounds, carried him from the river and laid him upon the bank.

I have been fairly beaten," Ferdia whispered, "but it is not right that I should die by your hand."

Across the ford, Rosemary and Jimmy watched in horrified silence as the victor bent and wept over his fallen brother. The great sobs tore through the air and his body shook with spasms of grief. But soon another sound reached them and panic-stricken, they saw a black line of men riding towards them.

"The Connaughtmen!" Rosemary cried. "They're attacking!"

"Quick,!" said Jimmy. "Drive the chariot across the river. I'll help Cuculann."

Jimmy splashed across the ford, shouting to Cuculann as

he ran, but when the warrior lifted his face it was wild with sorrow.

"Why should I leave when my brother lies dead before me?"

"It's not your fault!" Jimmy yelled, "He nearly killed *you*. Look, your own blood is pouring over him."

"What do I care if he wounded me?" Cuculann said in a lost voice. "He could have cut off my arm, my leg, my head for all I care. I should not have killed him. Our youth and childhood we spent together and now he is dead. Why should I go on living?"

Jimmy was almost crazy with frustration. When Rosemary drove the chariot up to them, Cuculann was cradling Ferdia's head in his lap and trying to stop the blood that trickled from his mouth.

"How I have hated this meeting, Ferdia," he moaned, rocking back and forth. "It was all a game till this. I have fought against the Tain in high spirits and happy courage, but it is all ruined now. All wrong. Your death should not have been part of it."

"Cucuc, you must come away now!" Rosemary urged. "Emer is waiting for you. You must go back to her."

His wife's name seemed to have some effect on Cuculann. He shook his head and looked around him in confusion.

"Why is Ferdia lying before me? What terrible dream is this?"

They pushed and pulled him till he was standing up, and together they dragged him to the chariot. Rosemary seized the reins and lashed out at the horses as the first Connaughtmen reached the ford. Spears whistled across the river, but the chariot was already speeding out of range.

"Whew, that was close," Jimmy said shakily.

When they looked back they saw that no one was following. The Connaughtmen had stopped at Ferdia's body.

Cuculann began to scream in agony as the movement of the chariot jarred his wounds.

"We've got to get back to Peadar," Rosemary said, terrified, "or he'll die right here."

When they drew up at the campsite, Emer ran to the chariot and clasped Cuculann in her arms.

"Help us!" she cried to the Druid, but Peter shook his head gravely.

"There is nothing I can do for him here. He is half-dead and his spirit has not moved to heal himself. We must bring him to the waters of Conaille to bathe him in the healing rivers."

Binding Cuculann's wounds with splints and bandages, they prepared the warrior as well as possible for the journey, but no matter how much cloth they wrapped around him, the blood still flowed freely. He swooned unconscious as they laid him on the floor of the chariot.

"The three of you will carry him to Conaille," the Druid told them. "You can take turns driving and tending him. I will go ahead and prepare for his coming. Emer knows the way you must travel."

They rode out in silence, each lost in their own thoughts and worry. Nothing could be said to Emer. She did not weep or waver, but her face was pale and hard as stone as she bent over the body of her husband.

Chapter Twenty-Six

 osemary and Jimmy sat on the bank of the River Finglas and dabbled their feet in the cool rushing water. A short distance away, Emer and her attendants were bathing Cuculann while the warrior protested mildly that he was 'being treated like a babe.' Though his body was crisscrossed with deep grooves and slashes, he looked much healthier after his days in the healing waters of Sas, the river of ease, Boann the river of strength, and Finglas, the river of spirit. Rosemary and Jimmy, on the other hand, were exhausted. Their hair was matted and bedraggled; their faces puffed with lack of sleep. The days and nights of Cuculann's recovery had been long and arduous for his friends. They were leaning against each other and dozing peacefully, when Peter joined them. Rosemary grinned as she looked at the Druid's worn face and dusty clothes.

"You're a wreck, Peadar. I suppose we are too."

"I will not argue the point," he said easily, as he splashed water on himself, "and that is why I have decided it is time to return home."

"Oh no," they said with dismay.

"But you can't leave now," Emer said, overhearing them.

She left Cuculann with the attendants and came to sit on the bank.

"I have sent word to my people. They are preparing a homecoming feast for all of you. You deserve it after these hard days."

"I'd love to see Cuculann's fort," Jimmy said eagerly.

"Please, Peadar," Rosemary pleaded. "Then we'll go."

The Druid raised his hands in surrender.

"I cannot dispute all of you. So be it. We will go to Dun Delga."

"But I am afraid, friends," Emer added, "I must lack in graciousness. We cannot all go by chariot. Cuculann should lie out and I will need the attendants to look after him."

"I'm all for a hike," Jimmy suggested, "if I get a good night's sleep beforehand."

"Me too," Rosemary chimed in. "It'll be a nice change from all the battles and excitement."

They set off the next morning with parcels of food and gourds of wine strapped to their backs. The Druid said little as they tramped through the countryside, but Rosemary and Jimmy chattered happily. The woodlands and meadows spread out before them, dappled with the bright shadows of sunlight. White hawthorn bloomed by yellow gorse on the hillsides; dark fern and goldenrod laced the streams and pools. Birds rustled in the hedgerows. Insects hummed beneath the warm grass.

"Mmm, this is like the early days of the march," Rosemary said dreamily, "when I rode with Maine."

"You liked him a lot, didn't you?" her brother said.

"It wasn't hard. If you weren't so prejudiced against

Connaughtmen you would have liked him too. Come to think of it, though, did you have your eye on anyone? What about Finn?"

"You gotta be kidding. Who needs all that competition? Anyway," he added, with a funny look on his face, "nobody could match a girl I saw once... when we came back here. Who was she Peter? And where did she come from?"

The Druid smiled wryly. "You are speaking of Ciobhan, the silver-eyed. She is a *speirbhean*, a sky-woman, and she lives in Sidh Seanarbh in the bright mansions of the North-world. She is a daughter of the Danaan tribe or the Sidhe as some call them."

"The gods?" Rosemary said in surprise.

"They call them gods here and the Irish of your world call them the Faery, but they are only another race in another world, though with more power than most. They are quite a nuisance moving in and out of the worlds, creating mischief as often as not. The Druids and the Sidhe are not good friends."

"Then Cuculann was right," Jimmy said. "He says his father is a god, one of the Sidhe."

"That is not surprising," the Druid replied.

When they had journeyed for several miles Rosemary and Jimmy began to grow tired. At one point Rosemary wished out loud that the Druid would change them into something that could travel faster. She had no sooner spoken than she was sorry, for he gave her a withering look.

"Shape-shifting is not something you do for sport. Magic is a serious art that should be used sparingly. You have two good feet to carry you and enough time to reach your destination."

"Sorry," she said meekly, and she made a mental note

not to become overfamiliar with the Druid. He was nicer than before, but he was still a prickly sort of person.

They reached Dun Delga on the Plain of Murtheimne by early evening and the welcome they received was like a hero's return. Coloured banners flew from the ramparts and Emer had called out her people to cheer them as they arrived. More roars of welcome greeted them when they entered the great hall. All Cuculann's men and ladies were gathered at the long tables. Huge logs burned in the hearth and servants rushed about with platters of meat and jugs of wine and ale. Acrobats capered in the middle of the floor, musicians wandered up and down the tables playing merrily, and everyone was singing and shouting and laughing. At the head of the first table, Cuculann sat propped up in a great chair with cushions all around him. He was dressed in finery, and though his face still wore the battered look of his struggles, his eyes lit up with joy when he saw them. He waved to the empty seats around him that had been kept in their honour.

"They will want to change first," Emer said in a wifely tone as she came to greet them. "If you begin your feasting early, husband, you will not survive the night."

"Ha!" Cuculann cried. "I have always wanted to give James the fullness of my hospitality and now I shall. Be quick, friend, and we will begin our merriment in earnest."

Emer led Jimmy and the Druid into the men's quarters where servants tended them with tubs of water and a fresh change of clothes. Rosemary was brought into Emer's own bower and while she bathed, Emer chose clothes and jewellery for her.

"Will this do?" Emer asked, lifting up a gown the colour of the evening sun.

Rosemary looked at the shimmering folds of reddish-orange silk.

"It's gorgeous. I love it!"

"You can have it," the girl said. "Now we'll have to find you some white gold to suit your dark hair."

"You sound like Finnabar," Rosemary said with a laugh, as she climbed out of the great metal tub. "Do you know her?"

"I met her once," Emer said, still busily sorting through her jewellery, "when King Conchobor made a friendship circuit of Ireland. A pretty girl, but she stands in the shadow of the Queen and it has left her empty-headed."

"You're right," Rosemary said. "But with a mother like that, who could blame her?"

When they rejoined the feast, they found Jimmy already settled in and telling jokes to Cuculann.

"Where's Peadar?" Rosemary asked.

"The high Druithin prefer their solitude," Emer explained, "but my husband has shown unusual care in the matter. He sent for Cathbad, our Chief Druid, who even now speaks with your friend in private chambers."

"Whatever makes him happy," Rosemary said.

A platter of sweetmeats was placed before her and she sipped red wine from a golden cup. In front of the table, three jugglers were doing their tricks while a tumbler, bedecked in bright ribbons, turned triple somersaults without stopping for breath.

Rosemary watched wide-eyed. "I have never been to a party like this in my life."

Emer laughed. "I do love feasting myself—all the dancing and eating and drinking, everyone singing and enjoying themselves, the pranks and playfulness. I wish you had been at my wedding, Rose." She was lost in her memories for a while and then she started to chuckle.

"Come on, tell me," Rosemary urged. "What's so funny?"

"I don't suppose Cucuc ever mentioned it. He has a sense of humour but not when it comes to himself."

"Well, what? What?" Rosemary demanded, laughing herself as the girl's giggles grew worse.

Emer glanced quickly at her husband, then inclined her head to Rosemary's and spoke in a low voice, still chuckling.

"You know of the right of the first night, Rose? No? It is a custom of our land. The King is the one who sleeps with a noble bride on her wedding night — don't look so shocked! — it has its good points. The King is always a great man and his blood, his children, strengthen and bind the people he rules over." Rosemary didn't look convinced, but Emer went on, "Conchobor is Cuculann's uncle and loves him well, but as King of Ulster he had the right to me on the first night of my marriage. He did not wish to, knowing full well how Cuculann felt about it. You can imagine?"

Rosemary nodded wryly as she thought of the fierce warrior's reaction to anyone sleeping with his bride.

"You'll never guess what happened!" Emer's eyes sparkled with merriment. "It is the law, and the King would at least have to lie in my bed for custom's sake. But even that drove Cuculann mad at the thought of it. He demanded witnesses to guarantee that nothing would happen. I spent my wedding night, Rose, near-smothered amongst the King, his eldest son, Cathbad the Chief Druid, and I don't know who else. The bed was crowded anyway. I didn't get a bit of sleep with all the elbowing and snoring. And there was Cucuc as well, in the next room, banging on the wall and insisting that I talk to him. Can you believe it?"

The girls spluttered with laughs and giggles. Emer made Rosemary pledge a vow of silence on the matter.

"What a strange life you lead," Rosemary said with wonder. "It sounds so exciting."

Emer shook her head and there was an edge of bitterness to her voice, "It wasn't always so. When I was in my father's house, I was treated like a slave. Such is the lot of all unmarried girls but I think my father was worse than most. I cooked, cleaned and waited upon his guests while he strove to sell me to the highest bidder. He was only interested in the brideprice, what my suitors offered for my hand in marriage. Cuculann courted me as early as ten years and I loved him from childhood, but my father feared and hated him. Through my father's trickery, Cuculann went away to Alba to learn the arts of war from their Queen. In his absence my father attempted to have me wed, but when I told each man I was promised to the Hound of Ulster they soon left me alone. I waited those long years for my beloved to return and when he did, he took me from my father's house by force.

"I was glad of it," she said fiercely. "When I found out how free I could be with my own house and servants, going in honour to the court of Ulster, and fighting behind my husband's shield—ah, the world became a good place to live in!"

"You fight beside Cucuc?"

"Not always. He prefers to fight alone. But it is a woman's right to fight beside her husband. I don't like it much, but when our fort is attacked I get angry and it feels good to fight back."

"I know what you mean," Rosemary said, remembering

Maeve's tent. "You must be so happy with Cucuc, Emer!"

She was sorry she put it so bluntly. Emer didn't answer and her eyes darkened. Rosemary sensed something hidden and deeply felt. It could be anything, she realized; the fear of Cuculann's death which might come so suddenly; the long, lonely absences when he was fighting; something Emer once said about his fondness for women. Rosemary searched for words to break the awkward silence when a clamour broke out at the entrance of the hall.

A warrior, dusty with travel, was beating his sword against his shield till it rang like a gong.

"To arms! To arms!" he cried. "Ulster, to arms!"

The warriors jumped up from the tables, their swords drawn. The music and singing came to an abrupt halt. Cuculann waved the man towards him, and the traveller ran to the head table, shouting.

"Ulster has arisen! The King gathers his people to march against Connaught!"

Cuculann's eyes shone as he turned to Jimmy.

"It is time, friend. The last great battle of the Tain is about to commence."

Cuculann was calling out orders to his fighting men when Peter joined them.

"Rosemary and Jimmy cannot go," he said quietly, ignoring the protests of the two. "My power wanes. We must leave."

There was a heavy silence as Rosemary and Emer, Jimmy and Cuculann, stared at each other unable to speak. The adventures they had shared rose up before them and they couldn't believe it was all over.

"I'm not going to say goodbye," Rosemary said tearfully to Emer, "but I guess that means I already have."

The two girls hugged and kissed as the tears flowed freely.

Jimmy and Cuculann looked stricken. Theirs had been the longest and closest friendship, and they were not ready to face its ending, for in their hearts, both knew they would never meet again.

"I won't forget you," Jimmy said. "Ever," and his voice broke.

Cuculann's eyes were dark with sorrow.

"It seems I am fated to live without my dearest friends. But I will remember always, Jim, the part you played in helping me on the Tain. Come, charioteer, a final farewell."

And they embraced each other as men and comrades-in-arms, fiercely and desperately.

Chapter Twenty-Seven

uculann's great hall was empty. The remains of the feast lay discarded on the tables. In the hearth, the flames flickered fitfully and collapsed into ashes. From the courtyard came the sounds of Cuculann and his men as they set off for battle. The uproar receded slowly into the distance and was gone. Rosemary, Jimmy, and the Druid stood together in the dim silence.

"It doesn't seem right, Peadar," Rosemary said sadly. "We've been here for all of it. Why not the final battle?"

"I wanted to be with him to the last," Jimmy said in a pained voice.

Peter sighed. "I am not insensitive to your disappointment, but I must fulfill my promise to protect you. My power no longer binds in this world. My time here has ended. I can no longer guarantee your safety."

Rosemary nodded, with unhappy resignation.

"Even if we could just *see* it," Jimmy suggested, undaunted.

A hint of amusement crossed the Druid's face and he looked thoughtful.

"Yes, that is possible, I suppose," he said, "I am still capable of changing your form."

Rosemary and Jimmy grinned at each other and waited expectantly.

"Very well," Peter said finally. "We shall go," and the three walked together from the hall.

As they passed through the great oaken portal, a gust of wind came rushing to meet them. The Druid's cloak billowed out like wide, black wings and they were lost in the soft folds of darkness. They felt themselves being carried upwards, suddenly buoyant and free, and then with a burst they fell out into the sky.

Jimmy and Rosemary cried out in fright.

"Why fear the heavens," Peter's voice called out, "when you are natives of it?"

"Oh yes," Rosemary laughed and it came out like a trill.

She soared into the skies. The blue land spread out before her, washed with the soft whiteness of the clouds. She stretched her wings and exulted in the splendour of wind and cloud.

Jimmy flew past her and touched her wing with his own.

"Can you talk?" he cawed.

"You sound funny, but I understand what you're saying," she crowed back.

They howled laughing at the sound of each other and as this resulted in a mad heap of cackling and cawing, they roared louder.

"I should have made you magpies," the Druid said, looming over them in the shape of the black raven. "Try to fly with dignity. You are both flopping around like hatchlings."

They smothered their bird-noises and fell into formation behind him. The countryside lay like a map below them, a brilliant shield of emerald crisscrossed by the thin silver veins of the ancient rivers. The three ravens glided downward till they were circling two low ridges of mountains.

"Gareich and Irgareich," Peter told them. "The Plain of Meath that lies between will be the arena of battle."

On the western ridge camped the Connaught armies, their tents and banners spotting the dark ground like patches of snow. To the east, the Ulster forces were crossing the steep paths of Irgareich. Troop after troop they marched, bright cloaks tossed back with careless pride, faces hard-set with grim expectation. They settled on the eastern ridge, lighting bonfires and pitching their tents. In the centre of the camp a great oaken chair was raised. Upon it sat a grey-haired man, stiff and furious. His face was flat and wide; a great brow loomed over his dark eyes. In a massive fist he held a sceptre that dangled with heavy golden apples.

"That is Conchobor mac Nessa," Peter said, "King of all Ulster."

Messengers could be seen scurrying between the camps and an uneasy truce was declared. The armies rested in their tents and the Plain of Meath lay silent between them.

The three ravens circled quietly in the sky, scanning the mountains for the first sign of movement.

"This waiting is making me nervous," Rosemary complained.

"That's the idea," Jimmy said knowingly. "Wait a minute! —look over there—do you see it?"

Below on the plain, a few stray cattle were wandering over the grass. The Ulster servants rushed out to claim them, as did the Connaught herdsmen. A quarrel erupted, shouts and threats rang out, and the men began to fight. It was the signal to war.

On the western ridge the Connaught warriors began the ritual of dressing for battle. War-cloaks unfurled, hair was bound, metal helmets glittered. The soldiers struck their shields in a steady drumming beat and the rattle of chariots rang through the high passes. But in the Ulster camp there was a strange quiet. Few men were astir and the tents remained closed like lidded eyes.

"Why aren't they moving?" Jimmy said anxiously.

"They are waiting for someone," Peter replied.

The Connaughtmen were already on the plain when a bloodcurdling roar echoed through the mountains. It was a cry of rage and vengeance, a call to war and victory. Like a clap of thunder, Cuculann's gleaming battle-car rode furiously into the Ulster camp. The reaction was instant. Men rushed from their tents naked. Weapons were seized and clashed together with terrific force. Chariots rumbled and horses stamped the ground. In a mass of howling rage, the Ulstermen poured onto the Plain of Meath.

"It has begun," said the Druid.

Musicians of war gathered at the battle lines. They raised great trumpets to their lips and blasted the air with cacophonous sound. War cries and screams of pain rose with the bellowing of the trumpets; grey metal glinted, dark blood spattered, and the ground churned beneath the tread of countless feet. Back and forth wove the battle, a massive tapestry of death and destruction. Thousands upon thousands fought on the plain. At times the Connaughtmen were in the ascendant, driving through the Ulster lines and forcing their foe to retreat and regroup. Then the Ulster army would rally and drive them back, breaking far into the western ranks.

High in the air, Rosemary and Jimmy watched the terrible spectacle in awe.

A ragged cheer rose from the Connaught army as Queen Maeve drove onto the battlefield. Like the goddess of slaughter herself, she howled with wild delight as her great sword flashed above the waves of men. Three times she drove the Ulstermen before her till their ranks broke apart in mad confusion. Then the King of Ulster entered the fray. He crashed into the battle on foot, his huge gold shield held like the sun before him. He roared like a maddened lion and his sword slashed and hewed with merciless vigour. Roused anew, the Ulster ranks swelled forward.

"Fergus! There's Fergus!" Jimmy cried. "Good luck, old friend! Take care!"

The exiled leader pressed through the writhing mass of fighters, his weapon rising and falling like a scythe in a field. He cut a bloody path through the Ulster lines as his grey head drew nearer to the golden shield of Conchobor the King. At last his mighty strokes were rebounding from the royal crest, and the two great warriors struggled together with ferocious enmity. They were matched in age and size, and both swords rang with the skill of countless campaigns.

Jimmy knew it was a death-fight and he circled anxiously above Fergus.

"Look out!" he screeched, as a big man stepped behind Fergus and pinned his arms.

Conchobor raised his arm to deal the final blow.

"Give up this fight, old men of Ulster!" the man cried, and with relief Jimmy recognized Conall Cernach. "Give up this madness!" he was shouting. "Will Ulster kings die while the Connaught witch laughs?"

Conchobor lowered his sword and with a curt nod turned to fight elsewhere, but Fergus struggled in Conall's arms and his face was red with fury.

"My weapon must be blunted!" he roared.

"Then attack the hills," his friend roared back, "or you will have to kill *me*."

Maddened, Fergus ran from the battlefield and charged like a bull at the hills. He tore up the grass and the stones and the earth, but his lust for blood was hardly spent. He returned to the battle, making his way once more towards the King.

A new cry rose from the Ulstermen as Cuculann rode onto the plain. His splendour and force outshone that of every king and warrior, but he did not stop to battle. With cold and steady purpose, he fought his way to Fergus till their swords met in the air with a resounding clash. Then Cuculann cried out in a clear voice.

"By the pact of truce and by the bonds of fosterage, yield to me, Fergus, as was promised at the ford. For your honour, you must yield. I demand it."

Fergus staggered back and slowly dropped his arm. Without a word, he fought to the edge of the plain and mounted his chariot. One by one his men followed suit, and the company of the Ulster exiles withdrew from the battle.

Jimmy watched Fergus's parting with relief.

"I'm glad he lived through this one. By the looks of things, not many will. Where has Cucuc gone?"

"He came only to rouse the Ulstermen and to demand Fergus's pledge," the Druid said. "Cuculann's destiny is to guard the borders till others come to take up their task. The last battle is not his. Cuculann's part in the Tain has ended."

With a sudden cry, Rosemary left them.

Flying wildly towards the familiar form, she found Maine surrounded by Ulstermen and fighting for his life. Without thinking, she darted in among them, flapping her wings and using her beak to scratch and maim. A dagger slashed at her face, a terrible pain gripped her. She felt the warm blood trickle over her eyes and everything turned red.

"Fool woman!" Peter cried.

He gripped her neck and pulled her upward into the sky. She ignored the pain and tossed her head till her vision cleared. Satisfied, she saw Maine reach his own lines to fight beside his brothers. As he joined the six other Maines, Rosemary thought triumphantly that Finnabar was wrong. She *did* know him from the rest.

"The brain of a bird is well suited to you, Rosemary Redding," the Druid scolded.

He had returned to human shape to tend the wounded bird and was carefully bathing the gash that ran across her forehead.

"Fair is fair. She owed it to him," Jimmy pointed out, as he preened his feathers.

"Well, she has received in turn what she gave. That was our agreement. There is a man who will go through life with the scar of a raven's talon over his left eye, and she will bear the mark of his dagger even in her own form."

"It doesn't hurt anymore, Peadar," Rosemary said.

When he didn't say anything she cocked her head and looked at him gaily. "I had to do it. After all, he was my first real love."

"I find that hard to believe," Peter said drily, but he was no longer angry. "It is a shallow wound and will heal quickly. Come, we must set out for home."

"But the battle?" they cried.

"See for yourselves."

They flew into the air, the Druid following them in his raven form.

It was over. The battlefield lay dark and murky. The fallen were heaped upon each other in great red cairns. To the east and to the west, the survivors were breaking camp and straggling homeward.

"Coming to the feast?" a crow asked Rosemary.

"Ugh!" she said.

"Follow me!" Peter cried, as he soared skyward.

Once more the land became a quilted network of green meadow and pale stream. Moor and woodland, valley and plain, swept away below them. They flew westward, passing the remnants of the Connaught armies, till they reached Cruachan Ai.

"There," Peter said, as they flew over Ai Plain. "There is the Brown Bull that Maeve coveted, and there is the White that she owned herself."

Below them on the royal plain of Connaught the two bulls met; Finnbennach, the White-Horned, monstrous and majestic, and Donn Cuailnge the Brown, a huge dark animal that snorted pillars of steam. A hairbreadth of time passed as the two bulls faced each other, their massive hooves pawing deep ruts in the ground, their eyes glowing red with savage hatred. Then they attacked. The earth shook with their thunderous stamps and roars. They gored each other's flesh, ripping hide and bone, spattering the plain with black spurts of blood. They charged and wheeled, horns locking, dust whirling. Their howls and bellows rang through the woods and hills of Ireland, and the land was a scene of turmoil and madness.

"It's awful," Rosemary murmured.

"Like the armies they will fight," Peter said cryptically, "and like the armies, neither will win. Such is the logic of war."

"Useless," Rosemary said finally, turning her face away. "There's no point to it at all."

"The time has come," the Druid said, and his voice seemed to be fading. "Nothing holds me to this world. We must return."

Upward he flew, straight into the path of the sun. They followed after, blinded by the glare of light. When they blinked to recover they found they were no longer in the sun-filled sky; they were standing in the sunshine of the fields around Drumoor.

Chapter Twenty-Eight

t was a grey, drizzly day and after an hour of looking out the kitchen window and dawdling over their tea, they knew the rain wasn't going to stop.

"A fierce lot of work'll be done today," Patsy said, shaking his head.

The past weeks had been spent bringing in the hay, but there were still a few fields left and Patsy wanted them finished by the end of August.

"Won't all that water ruin our haystacks?" Rosemary asked worriedly.

Her uncle smiled, "Well now and it shouldn't. We did a good job on them cocks. They're weatherproof, I'm thinkin'."

Jimmy gave his sister a scornful look.

"You dope. That's why we built them up like that. The rain runs off the sides and the inside stays dry."

"Oh shut-up, know-it-all," she said.

When Ella heard them bickering she decided it was time

to bring out the jigsaw puzzle. She spread it on the table and invited everyone to help. Patsy began methodically on the edges, as Ella studied the box lid that showed a picture of the Swiss Alps. Jimmy volunteered to do the sky, and then groaned when he had sorted out the blue pieces into a big pile.

"I'll be here forever," he said, but he was ready for the challenge as he drew his chair up to the table.

Rosemary grinned when she saw the three heads bend together over the puzzle.

"If you don't mind, Ella, I'd rather do some painting. I'll take it out to the barn so I won't make a mess."

Jimmy looked up eagerly. "Are you going to finish the one of me and…?"

"Maybe," she said, sticking out her tongue, "and maybe not."

The barn was nearly full with the hay they had brought in, but Rosemary was still able to sit in her favourite spot high in the rafters. The air was thick with the sweet, steamy scent of the dried grasses. Out through the loft, she could see the green fields drenched in a mist of rain. It was a quiet, pale scene, and she took out her watercolours to paint it. Lost in her work, she ignored whoever was climbing up the ladder and it was only when Peter sat beside her that she looked up.

"Oh hello," she said with a smile. "I thought you were Jim."

He looked down at her sketch and then out at the fields.

"You are a good artist. I saw this, when you were painting Drumoor. You go beyond what is there to the heart of the matter."

"Thank you," Rosemary said shyly. "I used to get confused about that. I was always mixed up with what I saw and what I wanted to paint. But since the Táin, I understand a lot more. It's like discovering the universe over again, except now I know all the other things in it. Gods and dreams and souls and other worlds."

"I, too, learned much from our journeying," Peter said.

"But we did nothing for you," Rosemary sighed. "We were so busy with the adventure we didn't even go back to Es Ruaid and visit the Harper. Will you go back again, do you think?"

Peter shook his head. "My power is finished. I cannot go back, and there is nothing to draw me there."

"I'm sorry about that," Rosemary said, but she couldn't help noticing that he wasn't. In fact, he seemed happier than she had ever known him to be.

"There is nothing to regret, Rose. I did not have to visit him. He came to me. Each day as I helped you, he moved closer, and now he is within me. What I sought I have found, and for that, I am content."

"Of course," Rosemary said. Why hadn't she seen it before? She had only to look at his face.

Her mind went back to the first time she met him, when he frightened her by the lake. This man beside her was not the same. The cold aloofness, the sharp lines of anger and torment, were gone. His skin was smooth, and suffused with the high, warm colour of a country man. His eyes had lost their peculiar whiteness, and now glimmered a soft, grey-blue. Though he was still withdrawn and a little shy, Rosemary decided he was a handsome, likeable young man.

"Of course," she repeated. "I understand now. It was all for you, wasn't it? That's the reason we went to the other world. And that's probably why we even came to Ireland in the first place! Like a web, drawing everyone in. Like the Harper's song."

"No, you are going too far there," Peter said, amused. "You might say the tune was played in my name, but certainly not all the threads nor all the patterns. And even if the song was woven for me to learn about myself and others, you could just as easily say that we were called together to take part in Cuculann's heroism, or to teach your brother to be less careless with his loved ones, or even to show you that there is more than the shallow, modern world.

"But the Song is never just for one, Rose. Never. There are no lone wanderers on the way to truth. It is a long and intricate search that calls for many journeys and many companions, and we weave each others' tunes inextricably and forever."

As Peter stood up to leave, he placed his hand on her shoulder.

"You didn't really want a cut and dried explanation, did you?"

"I guess not," she laughed. "That would only ruin the beauty of it."

"You see? I'm not the only one who changed."

A few days later, the letter that Rosemary and Jimmy had been dreading arrived. Their school term was beginning in two weeks and they had to return home to prepare for it. Their father had booked their tickets and they were to leave that Saturday.

"But I don't want to go back," Rosemary said, as she sat down to supper.

"Me neither," Jimmy groaned.

Their aunt and uncle looked at them sadly.

"Sure we don't want ye's to go either," Ella said, "but we can't be keepin' ye's from your schoolin'."

They stared dismally at their dinners. No one felt like eating.

"This is daft," Patsy broke in. "I've an idea. We'll have a great hooley in the kitchen and we'll be so tired from the singin' and dancin' that we won't notice the leavin' till it's over!"

The following night Ella had a turf fire blazing in the grate and the lace cloth on the table to show off her iced cakes, fruit tarts, sausage rolls and sandwiches. The neighbouring farmers began to arrive, dark and ruddy in their best suits, some with fiddles, flutes and melodians under their arms. The wives sat in a circle around Ella, praising her cakes and the idea of a party that brought them out of the house. The men drank glasses of ale and black porter, while the ladies sipped on hot punch. Rosemary and Jimmy mingled shyly, talking intelligently about heifers, crops and harvest weather.

"It's a pity now ye won't be here for the town festival," one of the farmers told Jimmy. "There'll be singin' and drinkin' and crack till ye don't know where you're at."

The musicians tuned up their instruments and began a lively medley of reels, jigs and hornpipes. Rosemary listened to them for a while, then sidled over to her brother.

"I'm going to fetch Peadar," she whispered. "I want to hear him play come hell or high water."

"Very aptly put," he said. "Good luck."

With his best smile, he turned to offer a plate of sandwiches to the ladies.

"Lovely boy," one of them said to Ella, and Jimmy smirked at his sister.

"Let me out of here," she groaned.

Rosemary slipped out the kitchen door and across the yard. Laughter and music trailed after her, and a golden light shone from the open windows. She found Peter in the barn reading a book by flashlight. His face was expressionless as he looked up at her, and she nodded towards the gay sounds of the party.

"Won't you come and say goodbye to us in true Irish fashion?"

"I don't mix well with other people," he said quietly. "I am sure you are aware of that."

"You mix well with Jim and me," she stated firmly. "We've been your companions through a wonderful adventure, Peadar, you can't refuse our friendship. We'll always think about you and we'll always be glad we met you."

He cleared his throat and said nothing. She could see that he was embarrassed and she wondered sadly if he were unused to kind words. She looked at the mandolin beside him, a delicate instrument of pale wood that curved like the neck of a swan. She held it out to him and said desperately, "I've never heard you play."

He took it from her and his long, slim fingers ran over the strings. A light, melodious sound rippled through the barn. It was strange to see such a big man leaning over a tiny instrument, but he held it gently like a father holds his child.

"What would you like to hear?" he asked her.

Rosemary closed her eyes with relief. When she opened them again, they sparkled with a wily mischief.

"Oh you can't just play for me, Peadar," she said innocently. "Your tunes shouldn't be just for one, you said so yourself."

She had caught him off guard. His laughter slipped out before he could recover. It was a pleasant sound, like leaves rustling in the wind, and she was glad she had heard it.

"Rose, you have Celtic blood in you," he said, shaking his head. "Such a trick would do Maeve no shame," and he stood up and followed her to the house.

Everything stopped abruptly when they stood in the doorway. The farmers and their wives stared in surprise. Here was Patsy's dark man whom no one knew and everyone talked about. Here was the 'queer fella' that made them uneasy even at a distance. Fear of the stranger crept into the room and the air was tense.

"Ah, you've come to play for us, Peter Murphy," said Ella softly, and she led him to a chair by the fire.

Without looking at the company, Peter bent over his mandolin and began to play. A small sigh rose from his listeners and there were nods and slow smiles of recognition. It was an air sad and sweet. It rippled over them like water, a cool stream of music that soothed and caressed. All closed their eyes and drifted with the sound. It was as if they were the instrument gathered up and played till their hearts sang.

One of the ladies began to hum quietly and then to sing. Rosemary nudged her brother as Ella's voice rose clear and high—

"The pale moon was rising
Above the green mountain,
The sun it was setting

Beneath the blue sea,
When I strolled with my love
By the pure crystal fountain,
That stands in the beautiful
Vale of Tralee.

She was lovely and fair,
Like the rose of the summer,
Yet it was not her beauty
Alone that won me,
No, it was the light
In her eyes ever shining,
That made me love Mary,
The Rose of Tralee." *

When the music ended, a quiet settled over the room and everyone looked pleased and lost and happy.

"Good man yourself!" one of the farmers shouted and they all clapped loudly.

Peter clutched his mandolin and looked around him shyly. Patsy handed him a glass of porter and the other musicians took up their instruments.

"Do ye know the Kesh Jig?" they asked him, "and Leitrim's Fancy? How about the Boys of Ballinamore?"

They played and played till their faces grew hot and pink. Jackets were removed and shirts opened, and the ale and porter flowed like the river. The men tapped their feet on the floor to keep the lively pace and one of the women got up to dance. More stepped out to join her and they danced the Walls of Limerick and the Seige of Ennis, the High Caul

*Irish traditional

Cap and the Humours Abandon. Rosemary watched them closely. The dancing was somehow familiar. When Ella caught her up and twirled her into the circles, the memory came to her with a sudden pang—a bright bonfire and the dance of the full moon.

Chapter Twenty-Nine

W hen the party was over and the last fare-wells had died out into the night, Rosemary and Jimmy volunteered to stay up and clean the kitchen.

"I'm glad Peadar played for us," Rose-mary said, when their aunt and uncle had gone to bed, "but I still feel depressed. I wish it didn't have to end this way."

"Yeah, I feel the same way," Jimmy grumbled. "I think I just don't want to go back to school."

They worked in moody silence till they were startled by a knock at the door. Peter stuck his head into the kitchen.

"Hurry up and meet me by the lake," he whispered, and disappeared again.

Rosemary and Jimmy looked at each other.

"Looks promising. Very promising," Jimmy said, and they rushed to finish what they were doing.

They knew something strange was happening as soon as they stepped outside the house. It was not an ordinary night. Everything was intensely still, as if the trees, the grass, the clouds in the sky, had caught the breath of the wind in their throats. There was a sharp, peculiar glitter to the air, like frost or crystal dew, and all was hushed and icy like a winter morning. Wide-eyed, Rosemary and Jimmy crept slowly up the hill. Neither wanted to speak. They felt dazed, lost in the magic they could sense around them. It pervaded every corner and space, and seemed to increase in strength, the closer they moved to Drumoor. When they reached the spinney that lay before the lake, they stopped and stared in wonderment. The trees sparkled like a silver fire raging across the meadow.

"It's so powerful, I can almost touch it," Rosemary whispered.

"All the other worlds," Jimmy said softly. "They must be very close."

They hurried through the shining trees and out onto the shore of the lake. Against the glowing sheath of the evening, Lake Drumoor lay like a still, black pool of ebony. Not a ripple marked the marble-smooth surface of the water and yet they could feel the presence of the lake as if it were alive and moving.

"Is that Peter?" Jimmy said suddenly, and his voice broke the silence like a loud echo.

Rosemary was startled, then she nodded.

The tall figure who stood by Drumoor was the source of light that was affecting everything. Though his hair was still dark and he wore the cloak of the Druid, the radiance of his person made him shine like a white candle against the gloomy lake. His face was calm and serene. A faint music played around him, like harp strings carried on a distant wind.

Rosemary looked into his eyes, as blue as a summer sea, and she smiled in recognition.

"I thought your power was finished," she said.

It was the same beautiful voice she had heard once before, that answered her.

"I am no longer a Druid," he said gently, "but I am a Harper. And I shall sing you a farewell in my own fashion. Draw closer, companions, and we three shall take our final journey."

He held each by the hand and they felt the light around him enfolding them like a cloak. As they turned to face the lake, he spoke quietly.

"Water belongs to the ages, the tears of humankind. It holds our secrets and the memories of all beginnings. It is life and we are given the gift of its mystery."

He began to sing; strange, exquisite words that moved inside them and called up power from the depths of their own being. They were suddenly aware, with a sharp and almost painful sense, of everything around them—every blade of grass in the meadow, every bird sleeping in the trees and hedgerows, every animal scurrying in the burrows of night. Their minds reached outwards, till they touched upon the sleepy farmhouse and their aunt and uncle lost in the peaceful world of dreams. Further again, they travelled down the roads of Ireland, over hill and field, meeting town after town...

"Come back," the Harper said, guiding them gently. "Come away from the world and look into the lake instead."

They did as he told them, calling their minds back to themselves, to focus their attention on Drumoor. With the power shining through their eyes, they could see beneath the surface of the water, deep into the heart of the lake where the shadow of reed and pike flickered over the sandy floor. Even as they touched the innermost part of the lake, they could sense Drumoor, like something alive, growing conscious of them. She seemed to reach out, gathering them to her watery embrace, drawing them down, like drowning souls, into her depths.

"Resist," the Harper urged quietly. "We wish to gain knowledge, not to be lost in it. Let her come to us."

Once again Rosemary and Jimmy controlled their power as the Harper directed, returning to themselves with deliberate effort. But now the lake followed, as if drawn to them in turn. Ripples broke across the surface, running noisily to the shore. The agitation grew. Waves began to rise and fall, white crests of foam bubbling over the dark water. They grew higher and higher, rising up like hills and then mountains, till they blocked out the stars of the night sky.

"Do not be afraid," Peter said. "She cannot harm us."

Rosemary and Jimmy held their breath as the water came crashing down towards them, but instead of sweeping them away, it raged around them, rushing in frantic circles like a towering cyclone.

"The eye of the hurricane," Rosemary whispered.

For the inner space that contained them was still and eerily silent. They were all eyes and mind caught and pinned in a whirlwind.

"Where do we go from here?" Jimmy wondered, and his voice echoed throughout the chamber.

"We are already moving," Peter replied. "We are inside what is moving just as you live on a planet that spins though you cannot feel it. Watch closely and you will see the journey we are taking."

For a long time nothing seemed to happen. Then shapes began to appear in the wind-wall. At first the images were blurred and unsteady, but they grew firmer till Rosemary and Jimmy were dazzled by the starkness and immensity. Like a magician's bright cloth, the panorama of the world was unfurled before their eyes. Stone by stone, under the labour of a million hands, they saw towers rise, cities grow, and empires spread. The lives of multitudes passed before them, birth, love and death repeated again and again. Sometimes the images were beautiful; a tall, noble people wandering over free plains; a wise king dispensing justice in his glittering hall; a small tribal race fishing patiently in the cold waters of a vast snowland. Other times the images were terrible; dark scenes of war and murder, hatred and cruelty. And in the pillage of time, as seas dried and mountains wore to plain, the towers and empires crumbled back to dust and new ones rose again. At times the teenagers recognized the scenes in awe; a wooden horse wheeled into a city by night; a man hung on a lonely cross atop a dark hill; an evil cloud rising from an island. But eventually human shapes and human events were lost in images that left them breathless and wondering; creatures of unknown shape and life; worlds of crystal, gas and fire; alien geography and alien lives. They knew they were looking at the histories, the stories, of countless worlds and races.

"It is coming," Peter broke into their thoughts. "You weave your own Song now."

The scenes were familiar again. It was not their world, but the world of the Tain. There was Cruachan Ai and the road to Ulster and the great Plain of Meath where they had seen the last battle. But the images were unsteady. They wavered and changed.

"Who?" Rosemary thought, "who's changing them?"

As she tried to make sense of the confusion, she suddenly saw Maine. Her love went out to him and his image grew in size and form. He was riding across a windswept plain, and Rosemary could see her own figure standing alone, lost and frightened. He reached out to her, lifting her high upon his horse, and wrapped her warmly in his great cloak.

"Ah yes," Rosemary whispered, remembering his strength, his gentleness.

She began to see what she had not seen before; Maine wandering through the dark forest of Es Ruaid, calling out her name, frantic for her safety; Maine in the camp of Maeve, struggling wildly in his bonds as the Queen railed against his disloyalty and two warriors stood over him with spears; Maine sitting alone in his palace at Cruachan, dreaming of a woman with long, dark hair.

"I know you love me!" Rosemary cried out to him. "But what can I do? I'm not in your world. You're not in mine. I'll never see you again!" and she was filled with a deep sorrow and the terrible ache of yearning and loss.

Jimmy, too, was lost in a tragic vision. There stood his friend, Cuculann, alone and bound to a great stone by the edge of the sea. Wounds gashed his mighty body and his eyes were dark with the misery of defeat. He gripped his long sword in a dying hand and awaited the last moment of his life.

"You can do better than that," the Harper chided them. "Worlds wait to be created by dreams. You are both young, have you no hope in your hearts?"

Rosemary and Jimmy fought against their despair, searching in their minds for other thoughts and memories.

Now Jimmy remembered something that Cuculann had

told him a long time ago. As he looked again at the image of his friend, he saw that the warrior was not alone. By Cuculann's death-stone stood a shining figure, a tall god-man with a silver spear that touched the sky.

"I am here," Lug mac Ethenn whispered to his son. "I have come to bring you home."

"I see it now!" Jimmy cried suddenly. "I understand the Song! There is no ending. It goes on and on. Just like he told me. There are other places. There'll be other times. We *can* meet again. He's my friend, forever!"

Rosemary heard her brother's cry and the same knowledge that had come to Jimmy rose in her also.

"I see it too!" she said, laughter breaking through her tears. "It was there all the time, only I didn't put it together. The other worlds, the gods, dreams and souls, the Druid and the Harper—they all point to the same thing!" And with the hope-filled song of infinity, a new vision came to her. A night sky sprayed with stars and the moon glowing like a huge opal. Flames burning on a hilltop and the shadows of young lovers dancing round the fire. She could see herself, hand clasped in Maine's, leaping high over the red, burning embers. She was laughing, breathless, eyes shining, as Maine caught her up in his arms.

"It is forever, Rose! By the bond of moon and fire, we belong together, through all time, through all the ages!"

"It *is* forever," she repeated, as the image flared around her. "I'll meet you again, beloved. Again and again."

The visions faded away and Peter's voice was tired but triumphant.

"Now I can sing you mine."

They could see a dark figure moving furtively in the shadows. He seemed to be searching for something, and he journeyed deep into the caves of the earth and high over the furthest mountain peaks. Time passed, and though he grew older and appeared stooped and broken, his wandering continued and he was always alone. The places he visited became darker and more terrible; great, empty tombs, lost cities, and wild, forsaken regions shunned by man. Then two smaller figures joined him. His image straightened, but there was still anger and tension in his limbs. He tried to escape, but the two were always near. Slowly he began to change. A dim light kindled inside him and steadily grew, till he was consumed in a magnificent blaze of fire.

They knew it was the Druid's tune and it made them sad and proud.

"Who seeks alone," sang the Harper, "is lost in the darkness of self. I have called up knowledge for my companions, and through them I have found truth."

A final image rose before them, Lake Drumoor in the paling light of dawn. The Harper stood by the water's edge, his back towards them. There was a flash of gold and an unfurling of black, and the lake rippled in slow spirals as something sank beneath its surface. When Peter turned to Rosemary and Jimmy with a warm smile of friendship, they realized that they were no longer looking at an image. Everything was real and they were standing in their uncle's meadow. They stood in rapt silence, so filled with visions and memories that their hearts sang. Peter walked from the field without a word and still they didn't move. Then Jimmy shook himself awake and grinned.

"That's typical. He didn't even say goodbye."

Rosemary raised her eyes to the sky.

"You blockhead, of course he did."

Historical Note

The Tain Bo Cuailnge, the "Cattle-Raid of Cooley", is Ireland's national epic myth. After centuries of oral story-telling, it was written down in Old Irish and survives today in medieval manuscripts of the 12th and 14th centuries. The Tain tells the tale of the invasion of Ulster by the armies of Queen Maeve of Connaught and the single-handed defence waged by the young warrior-hero Cuculann.

The story is set in pagan, Iron-Age, Celtic society dated anywhere from before Christ up to the 5th century A.D. Life, then, was centred on small tribes ruled by chieftains and based on an economy of farming and cattle-raising. As in the "Heroic Ages" of ancient Greece and Rome, the myths and poetry of this time accent the heros and deeds of the warrior class. (Cuculann can be seen as an Irish Her-cules.) At that time, also, gods, magic, and superstition were a normal part of life and the sacred caste of Druids wielded a strong influence over the affairs of the tribe and the activities of Kings, Queens, and warriors.

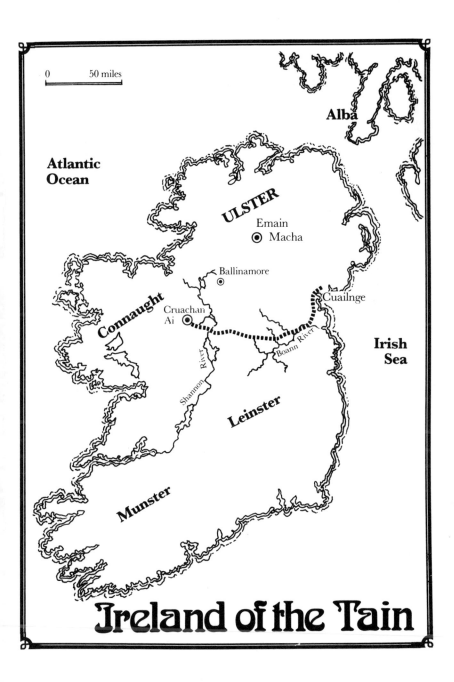

0   50 miles

Alba

Atlantic
Ocean

ULSTER

Emain
◉ Macha

Ballinamore
◉

Connaught

Cruachan
Ai ◉

Cuailnge

Shannon River

Boann River

Irish
Sea

Leinster

Munster

Ireland of the Tain

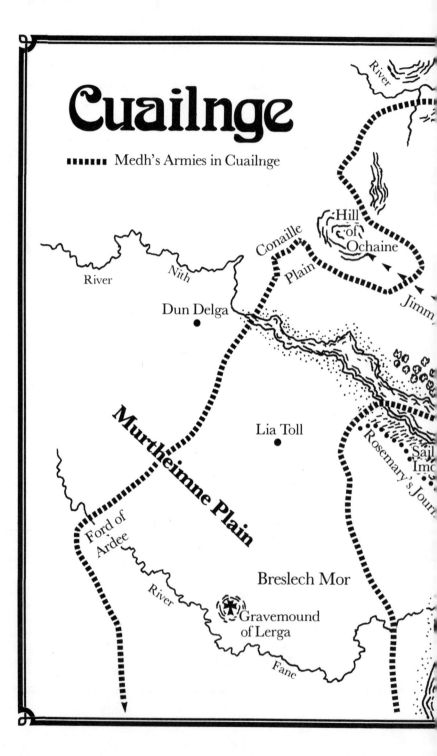

Cuailnge

▪▪▪▪▪▪ Medh's Armies in Cuailnge

River

Conaille

Hill of Ochaine

Plain

River   Nith

Jimm

Dun Delga

Lia Toll

Rosemary's Jour

Sail
Imo

Murtheimne Plain

Ford of
Ardee

Breslech Mor

River

Gravemound
of Lerga

Fane

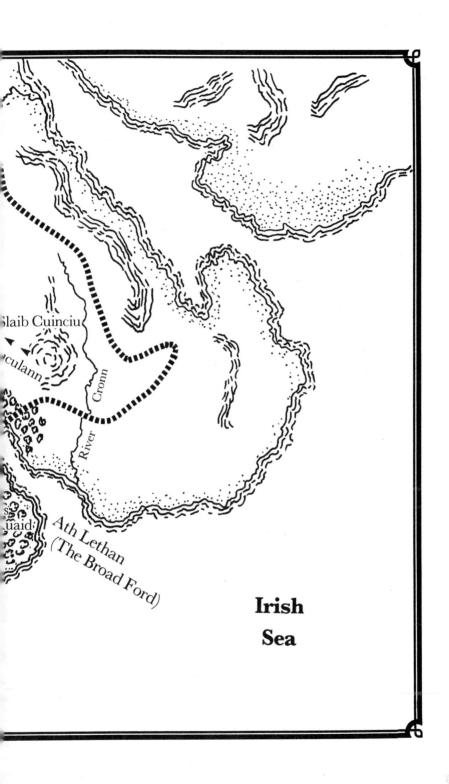

Slaib Cuinciu

Culann

River Cronn

uaid

Ath Lethan
(The Broad Ford)

Irish

Sea